**"So you're backing
out of the deal?"**

"It wasn't the deal I made, and you
know it!" Marcus had tricked her.

"You said I could Braille you if I
discarded the sunglasses you've
taken such an aversion to."

"I meant my face, not my body!" Olivia
gasped.

"Pity." Marcus's expression hardened.
"You're probably too thin for my
tastes, anyway," he added insultingly.

It was even more of an insult than he
knew. Olivia remembered clearly the
voluptuous wife he had preferred to
her long ago.

She looked to see the bitterness
etched in his harsh face. And those
damned glasses—how she hated
them! But enough to withstand
Marcus's hands on her body? "All
right!" she snapped. "You can Braille
my body, too."

"I'm not that desperate," he
dismissed rapidly.

Books by Carole Mortimer

These books may be available at your local bookseller.

For a list of all titles currently available,
send your name and address to:

Harlequin Reader Service
P.O. Box 52040, Phoenix, AZ 85072-2040
Canadian address: P.O. Box 2800, Postal Station A,
5170 Yonge St., Willowdale, Ont. M2N 5T5

CAROLE MORTIMER

everlasting love

Harlequin Books

TORONTO • NEW YORK • LONDON
AMSTERDAM • PARIS • SYDNEY • HAMBURG
STOCKHOLM • ATHENS • TOKYO • MILAN

For
John and Matthew

Harlequin Presents first edition August 1984
ISBN 0-373-10716-1

Original hardcover edition published in 1984
by Mills & Boon Limited

CHAPTER ONE

'READY, Olivia?'

Olivia sighed, moving to open the door to admit Natalie Irving, a young and pretty girl of seventeen, with long golden hair. 'Are you sure you and Rick wouldn't rather go on your own?' she frowned. 'I can easily go shopping for the afternoon. There are lots of things I——'

'Now don't be silly,' Natalie dismissed, coming further into the bedroom. 'Is this your costume?' She held up the emerald-coloured bikini, leaving the black one-piece suit on the bed where they had both been laid out for Olivia's examination.

'The black——'

'Too old-fashioned,' the young girl dismissed with a wrinkle of her nose, and rolled the bikini in the towel, tucking them both under her arm, sighing as she saw Olivia still hesitated. 'You know Rick feels easier when you're around,' she encouraged softly.

Olivia sobered as she thought of her patient, her green eyes thoughtful, a frown marring her usually smooth brow. She was seven years the other girl's senior, although she didn't feel it when Natalie bossed her about in this way! She didn't look it either, in the clinging black vest-top and wrap-around green and black skirt, her legs long and bare, her feet thrust into loose sandals, her hair a mass of red-gold curls, her face youthfully beautiful, even if the chin was a little too determined.

'I'm not sure that's good for him,' she said quietly. 'I'll be gone in a couple of days now that Rick is well again. I don't think he would still depend on me.'

'He doesn't,' Natalie dismissed with a confident laugh. 'He likes you, and he's grateful. Most nurses would jump at the chance of an afternoon lazing by the pool—wouldn't they?' she prompted teasingly.

Yes, they would. And after weeks of caring for Rick Hayes, of making him believe he could walk again, of convincing him that he wasn't going to be a cripple all his life, an afternoon doing nothing but sunbathe and swim was exactly what she needed.

'But wouldn't you and Rick rather be alone?' Still she hesitated about accepting the invitation. The Hayes family, mother and father, Rick, and his young sister Dawn, had all been very kind to her during the three months she had been Rick's private nurse after he was discharged from hospital following a serious car crash. But there had to be a limit to that kindness, and surely intruding on Rick's date with his long-time girl-friend Natalie was that limit.

Natalie didn't seem to think so. 'We can hardly be alone with thirty other people,' she said dryly.

Olivia's eyes widened. 'Is that how many will be there?'

'About that,' the young girl nodded.

'Then perhaps I ought to go, on a professional level,' she murmured thoughtfully. 'It will be Rick's first time among so many people, I don't know how he'll react to people seeing his limp.'

'He'll be fine,' Natalie assured her. 'Okay, so he'll never play football for England—he never could play the game anyway,' she dismissed lightly. 'A little old limp isn't going to effect his becoming an architect, and that's all he's interested in.'

'Besides you,' Olivia teased, knowing the young couple intended getting engaged on Natalie's eighteenth birthday.

The younger girl grinned. 'That goes without saying.'

'Modest with it!' Olivia laughingly followed Natalie down to the car where Rick sat impatiently waiting for them.

'I was going to send out a search party,' he moaned as he drove out on to the country road. 'I'll never know what you women find to talk about all the time!'

'Men, sweetheart,' Natalie taunted.

'I hope you meant that in the singular?' he returned with mock jealousy.

'I wouldn't want to make you conceited,' his girl-friend returned haughtily.

Olivia sat in the car listening to their lighthearted bantering, smiling to herself. She was going to miss this family, every mad, lovable member of it, from the absentminded Clara, practical joker Eric, handsome Rick, self-assured Natalie, to shy Dawn, the latter slightly overshadowed by the other extroverts in her family. Three months of sharing their big rambling home was a long time to spend in close living with anyone, and the lack of a close relationship with her own parents had made her appreciate this loving and loved family all the more.

But soon it would be over, only another five days and she would be leaving to take care of her next patient, an elderly woman who had fallen and broken her leg, needing nursing care for her first few weeks at home. She would be sorry to leave the Hayes family; she had become very fond of them all. Becoming emotionally involved was a hazard of nursing she had never quite managed to overcome, and she doubted she ever would.

But she hadn't left this family yet, the sun was shining, Rick and Natalie were very much in love, a wonderful glow emanating from them that made her feel included in their happiness at being alive.

Several boisterous teenagers were already in the pool when they arrived at the Grayston home, and

Olivia was at once included in their laughing group, despite her age difference from most of them.

Happily Rick showed no selfconsciousness about wearing bathing trunks, though his legs were still badly scarred from the accident, the limp quite noticeable on one of them. But he was mentally a well-adjusted young man, and had handled the inactivity during the first months after the accident with calm acceptance, only occasional panic setting in as he doubted he would ever walk again. But his progress from not being able to walk at all to walking unaided now had been a rapid one considering the extent of his injuries, and he was coping with his limp with the same maturity that he had handled the rest of his illness.

But as Natalie had said, it was Olivia's afternoon off, and after assuring herself that Rick was really all right, she lay back on a lounger to enjoy it, very slender in the emerald-green bikini Natalie had insisted she bring in preference to the more sedate black, dark sunglasses pushed on the bridge of her nose hiding eyes the same colour as the bikini.

'Like to borrow some sun-tan lotion?' a young female voice offered.

Olivia sat up, grateful for the offer; she had already felt the sun's rays beginning to burn her delicate skin. 'Thanks,' she smiled, pushing her sunglasses up into the riot of red-gold curls.

'Olivia!'

She looked curiously at the young girl sitting on the lounger beside her. She didn't look familiar; her long dark hair was pulled back to be secured in an impish ponytail, her face young and pretty, her grey eyes wide in surprised recognition. Grey eyes . . .?

Olivia's interest quickened as she studied the young girl, the stubborn chin, the determined mouth, and those shockingly familiar grey eyes. 'Sally . . .?'

'Yes!' the young girl cried excitedly. 'How are you?

You look well. What are you doing now? Oh, of course, you came with Rick, so you must be the nurse he talks so highly of. Are you—Did I say something funny?' she frowned as Olivia began to smile.

Olivia's smile deepened. 'Well, so far you've answered every question you've asked.' Added to which, if she didn't smile she might cry! She had thought the Hamilton family were well out of her life, and to see Sally again, after all this time, was startling to say the least.

'Sorry,' Sally gave a rueful grimace. 'It's just such a surprise to see you like this.'

That had to be the understatement of the year! 'How have you been?' Olivia asked politely.

'Fine,' the young girl nodded.

'And your father?' her voice cooled somewhat.

Sally anxiously searched the bland expression on her face. 'He's well too. Working too hard!'

'He always did.' Olivia sounded brittle, fighting images of Marcus from her mind. She hadn't thought of him for weeks, and she wouldn't think of him now, wouldn't allow this chance meeting with Sally Hamilton to disrupt the even tenor of her life.

'You haven't seen him since——'

'Not for some time, no,' she cut in sharply. 'You mentioned something about sun-tan lotion just now,' she abruptly changed the subject.

'Oh—of course,' the young girl flushed, handing her the plastic bottle containing the brown lotion, watching as Olivia began to smooth it on her creamy skin. 'Don't you want to talk about Daddy?' she finally probed after several silent minutes.

Olivia didn't look up, her breathing becoming shallow. 'Is there anything to say?' She knew the question was put in such a way that it was a complete contradiction of itself, that she very much wanted to hear about Marcus, would accept any little crumb of information she could get about him. And as his daughter, Sally was guaranteed to know plenty about Marcus.

'I somehow thought—I just never expected you and Daddy to break up like you did. You seemed—well, he really liked you,' Sally finished awkwardly, her gaze questioning.

'I'm sure he did,' Olivia agreed with some bitterness. 'But there was you—and your mother.'

'Oh yes—Mummy,' Sally grimaced.

Olivia's eyes widened at this reaction. 'You never used to feel that way about her,' she frowned, remembering well how Sally had cavaliered her mother.

'People change,' the girl shrugged. 'It was six years ago, I was only twelve, still a child really.'

And yet that child had helped to push the wedge between Marcus and herself, Sally's obvious aversion to any female but her mother in her father's life making Olivia's relationship with Marcus impossible. And that was before Ruth came back!

'I didn't understand the situation,' Sally added lamely.

'Of course you didn't,' Olivia agreed brightly. 'I'm not really sure that I did. I was only eighteen myself then.'

'But you loved Daddy!'

'I may have thought I did——'

'I'm sure you did,' Sally insisted vehemently.

'Maybe for a time,' Olivia acknowledged tightly. 'But a man in your father's position couldn't afford to be involved with an eighteen-year-old. After all,' she added tautly, 'he was Chief Surgeon even then.'

'He still is,' Sally nodded. 'At a different hospital—bigger.'

'Yes.' It had to be. Marcus would be thirty-nine now, and he had always been destined to be at the top of his profession; it sounded as if he had made it. 'And your mother, how is she?' she heard herself ask, her breath held in her throat as she waited for the younger girl to tell her how happy her parents were together, that they perhaps even had more children.

'Mummy?' Sally gave her a startled look. 'But don't you know?' She sounded puzzled.

Olivia frowned. 'Know what?'

'My mother died three years ago.'

She swallowed hard, shocked in spite of her usual calm composure. 'I—I had no idea,' she shook her head. 'I'm sorry,' she added dully.

Ruth Hamilton had been dead for three years, and she hadn't even known about it! That meant that Marcus had been on his own for all that time—or did it? Marcus was hardly the type to be alone for any amount of time, hadn't the two of them met during a temporary separation from his wife Ruth. And hadn't she been discarded just as quickly as soon as Ruth decided to come back! No, whatever hopes she might have had about Marcus for all these years, there had never been a chance of the two of them ever getting back together again. Although she felt sure there would be a woman in his life.

'Your father's married again?' she queried softly.

'Only to his work,' Sally replied dryly. 'He'll always be married to that.'

'Yes.' Olivia stood up with jerky movements. 'I think I'll go in for a swim,' she told the girl brightly. 'It's been nice seeing you again. 'Bye!' and she ran to the edge of the pool.

'Oh, but——'

Olivia didn't wait to hear any more, but dived smoothly into the clear blue water, welcoming its coldness, doing several laps of the pool before she even dared to look up again. Sally had gone from the adjoining loungers and was listening rather absently to a young man as he talked to her at the other end of the pool. Olivia levered herself out on to the side of the pool before hurrying to the changing-rooms, anxious that Sally shouldn't speak to her again.

Sally seemed to have matured into a very nice young lady, and yet six years ago she had been totally spoilt, and completely possessive of her father. Marcus had responded to that possessiveness with gentleness and understanding, but Olivia hadn't been able to cope with the young girl's rudeness quite so calmly. And even that hadn't been all Sally's fault; Olivia knew she had been too unsure of Marcus and his interest in her to defend herself against any barbs she might receive, too vulnerable and uncertain in her youthful love of him.

'Ah, good, you're ready to leave.' Natalie met her outside the changing-rooms. 'I hope you don't mind, but Rick has had enough for one day.'

All Olivia's concern was instantly for her patient, her own troubled thoughts forgotten. 'I should have thought of that——'

'Of course you shouldn't,' Natalie laughingly dismissed. 'He's an adult, he should know when it's time to go. And luckily he does. If you want to stay on I'm sure I could get someone to drive you back later——'

'No, I'm ready to go.' Her voice was sharper than usual, and she sensed Natalie's questioning look. 'I— The sun is very tiring,' she invented.

'Of course,' Natalie agreed sceptically. 'None of our friends were making nuisances of themselves, were they? I know some of the boys——'

'No, no, it isn't that.' Olivia assured hastily. 'It really is just tiredness.'

'You seem—upset about something?' the other girl persisted.

Was she so transparent? She hadn't thought she was, had thought she had built up a protective shell these last few days. A few minutes' conversation with Sally Hamilton, unwilling thoughts of Marcus thrust upon her, and her carefully controlled veneer had been shattered; Natalie sensed it, and now she was forced to acknowledge it to herself too. 'Tired,' she insisted firmly, following the other girl out to the car.

Rick frowned at her in the driving-mirror as they drove back to his home. 'Are you all right?'

'She's tired,' Natalie answered him.

His brows rose. 'You seemed to be resting when I looked at you. You were talking to Sally for quite some time.'

Olivia moistened her dry lips. 'She didn't ever come to the house while you were ill, did she?' she queried in a casual voice—too casual?

'Only once, I think,' Rick answered thoughtfully. 'It was probably your day off.'

'Oh, that one,' Olivia teased.

'Cheeky!' he grinned at her.

'Well, Olivia's days away from you haven't exactly been numerous,' Natalie reasoned.

'Go on, she's loved every minute of it.'

'Yes, I have,' she agreed warmly.

'Don't tell him that,' Natalie groaned. 'He'll be unbearably conceited about it.'

'And I thought you loved me?' he groaned.

'I do—sometimes,' she added coolly.

'Thanks!'

'I think you asked for that one, Rick,' Olivia laughed.

'Probably,' he grimaced.

Oh, she was going to miss this family! That fact was brought home to her even more as she ate a lighthearted meal with them that evening. Clara and Eric had insisted that she ate all her meals with them, treating her like another daughter they had suddenly acquired. Five more days and she would be leaving this

happy family group to take care of an elderly lady, and
the contrast between the two households would be
extreme. But she had chosen her profession, enjoyed
it, and if she was sometimes lonely then that was her
fault; the offer of boy-friends had been there often
over the years. But none of those men had ever
measured up to Marcus——

Marcus! Couldn't she get away from thoughts of
him today? It would seem not, as she heard Rick
mention Sally Hamilton to his father.

'Sally's back from Switzerland,' he told him.

'And Marcus?' Eric enquired.

'I think he's back too. I know her grandmother is
with her,' Rick remarked casually.

Sybil—Sybil Carr, Marcus's mother-in-law. Olivia
had met the other woman, had found her reception to be
frosty, although in the circumstances that was perhaps
understandable. The absent Mr Carr was a wealthy
businessman—what else, with Ruth's air of breed-
ing!—and he had been in America on business during
the brief months Oliva had been in Marcus's life.

'To stay or just to visit?' Clara asked interestedly.

'To stay, I think,' her son shrugged.

'Poor Marcus,' Clara said softly. 'Still, I don't
suppose there's much point in Sybil staying in
Switzerland now that Gerald is dead.'

So Sybil Carr was now a widow. Olivia somehow
couldn't envisage the haughtily sophisticated woman
as a grieving widow, stricken by her loss. No, that role
didn't suit the other woman at all.

'I'm sorry, Olivia,' Clara spoke to her in her gentle
voice; she was a prettily vague woman who somehow
managed to carry on in her own sweet way, never
hurting anyone or anything, and her family drew peace
from her serenity. Olivia liked the older woman
immensely. 'It's rude of us to discuss people you don't
know,' she smiled her apology.

'Olivia met Sally today,' Natalie put in, spending more time here than in her own home with her parents.

'Did you, dear?' Clara gave one of her vague smiles. 'She's a nice girl, isn't she?'

'She seemed to be,' Olivia nodded, then stood up to excuse herself. 'I have some reading to do before I go on to my next case.'

'Of course, dear,' Clara nodded understandingly.

Olivia lingered at Rick's side. 'Will you be all right?'

'Why?' he grinned. 'Are you offering to come and tuck me up in bed later?'

'She'd better not!' his girl-friend threatened.

'Why not? She has done for the last three months,' he mocked.

Natalie looked up at her appealingly. 'Olivia——'

'He's only teasing you,' she smiled at the other girl. 'Most of that time I *put* him in the bed, not tucked him into it!'

She left the room to the sound of teasing laughter and mocking comments, all of them directed at Rick. And at least now the subject of Sally and Marcus had been forgotten.

But not by her. It was all back with a vengeance, all the love, the disillusionment, and finally the pain.

Being a nurse had seemed so romantically glamorous when she was eighteen, a sort of modern-day Florence Nightingale, soothing a patient's brow and he or she instantly recovered, and every doctor just longing to fall in love with, and marry, a nurse.

Reality had been less of an ideal, and after six months' training, three months of it actually working on a ward, the other three in the classroom, Olivia had been forced to acknowledge that there was little romance attached to the profession, only gruelling hard work, and even the lowliest doctors treated her as being beneath their notice, romantically or otherwise. Oh, she had no doubt that a few of the senior nurses had relationships with some of the doctors, but they rarely, if ever, led to anything permanent.

Her first ward had been a children's, and while some of the children there had been very ill, on the whole it had been an enjoyable time, and death had never touched her.

Her second ward had been something else completely—female medical, a mixture of all ages over twelve, although the younger patients seemed to recover quicker and leave after only short stays with them. Some of the older patients, their healing process not always as healthy, made much longer stays.

It was in this way that she had become fond of Mrs Bateson, a woman in her seventies. It had become part of Olivia's daily routine to spend several minutes out of her busy day talking with Mrs Bateson about the olden days, her fifty years of marriage to Bert, her six children, twenty grandchildren, and four great-grandchildren. Emily Bateson was fascinating to talk to, to listen to, and with the lack of a closeness to her own parents Olivia became very fond of the elderly lady.

In fact the first time she had ever seen Marcus she had been standing at Mrs Bateson's bedside talking to her about the expected visit from her frail husband, for the old lady was never happier than when her husband was going to keep her company for a time, most of her day spent in bed because of her illness.

Emily looked down proudly at the gold band on her wedding finger, worn thin with time. 'Never been off my finger since the day Bert put it there,' she glowed.

Olivia found the love the elderly couple still had for each other, even after fifty years of marriage, very beautiful to witness. During visiting time the couple would hold hands like two teenagers, and they never seemed to be angry with each other. Mr Bateson was always bringing a small gift for his wife, even if it was only a small container of talcum powder.

'Curtains, Nurse,' Sister Marton said briskly from behind her.

Olivia gave a guilty start and turned selfconsciously, only to collide with the person standing directly behind her. 'Sorry,' she murmured, her lids fluttering up to meet frosty grey eyes, no sympathy for her embarrassment in the hard face as the man brushed past her to begin examining Mrs Bateson.

She beat a hasty retreat, joining the other nurses who had disappeared into the clinic-room at the advent of a consultant.

'I see they've brought in the big man himself,' Katy Barnes said softly.

'Who is he?' Olivia demanded of her fellow student-nurse in a whisper. As the two most junior nurses they were still a little shy about joining in conversations with the older girls.

'Marcus Hamilton!' Katy told her, scandalised that she hadn't recognised him. 'Gorgeous, isn't he?'

He certainly was, as handsome as he was reputed to be. Olivia had heard the hospital gossip about the attractive Mr Hamilton, the hospital's top surgeon, and having now seen him she had to agree with the majority view—he was devastatingly handsome! He was very tall, with dark brown hair, kept short and tinged with grey at his temples, the face strong and dominating; the grey eyes piercing, the nose long and straight, his mouth stern and forbidding, the jaw angled squarely. As a consultant, high above the level of a doctor, he wore no white coat to identify him, and his dark three-piece suit was superbly tailored to his powerful body, his legs long and muscled.

He was breathtaking, and even Mrs Bateson was later full of her 'handsome young doctor', although

Marcus Hamilton was obviously in his early thirties. That must have seemed young to Mrs Bateson, although it seemed very mature to Olivia.

After that initial encounter she saw Marcus about the hospital several times, occasionally with other consultants or doctors, but usually alone. He seemed a very solitary man, his aloofness from the rest of the hospital staff making him a prime target for gossip, although it was the same aloofness that made it difficult to find out too much about him. And Olivia was very interested in knowing about him, suffering from her first crush ever on an older man.

It was one day two weeks after their first meeting that Marcus actually spoke to her—and in the circumstances she would rather he hadn't.

Mrs Bateson had been looking anxiously at the open ward door all during visiting time, and finally it was Marcus Hamilton who came through it and walked to her beside, pulling the curtains about the bed himself, emerging ten minutes later, when all the visitors had gone from the ward, with his face set in harsh lines.

'Nurse!' he called Olivia over from where she had been hovering, worried by this strange turn of events.

'Yes?' She looked up at him with wide green eyes, so nervous she was shaking. 'Sir,' she added belatedly.

He seemed not to notice the drop of etiquette. 'Would you go in with Mrs Bateson for several minutes? I don't want her to be alone, one of her daughters should be in soon.'

'Er—Of course,' she looked startled. 'What——'

'Her husband has just died.'

Olivia didn't wait to hear any more, but hurried to the elderly lady's bedside with a strangulated cry of pain. The light had gone from Mrs Bateson's eyes, and all she could do was clutch on to Olivia's hand as if she never wanted to let go. She didn't even cry, although Olivia felt as if *she* needed to. Sister Marton looked in a few minutes after Marcus had left, nodding approvingly before quietly leaving again.

Time seemed to stand still after that, the time passing although neither of them seemed aware of it; there was no conversation between them, the elderly lady seeming to draw comfort from Olivia being at her side.

Suddenly Mrs Bateson spoke. 'We always said we wanted to go together,' she murmured softly.

'Mrs Bateson——'

'I can't go on without Bert,' the old lady told her sadly. 'One day you'll understand, Olivia,' she used her first name without conscious thought, although Olivia couldn't remember ever telling it to the other woman, the familiarity not really being allowed. Not that she thought anyone would object in the circumstances! 'I've loved Bert all my life, and without him I just don't want to live.' She lay very still in the bed.

'Mrs Bateson, you mustn't talk this way——'

'Nurse King!'

Olivia looked up to see Marcus Hamilton standing just outside the slightly opened curtains that were still pulled about the bed, gently releasing her hand from Mrs Bateson's to go to him. 'Yes, sir?' she queried softly, amazed that he knew her name.

'How is she?' His expression was intent.

It was a strange question for a consultant to ask a junior nurse—after all, he was the expert. 'Er—she's very shocked—sir,' she moistened her lips in her nervousness. 'Although she seems to be coming out of that now,' she frowned her concern.

'Yes?' Marcus Hamilton sensed her worry.

'She's talking about dying.'

'God! Sorry, Nurse King,' he was at once the controlled consultant once again, 'I'm going in to talk to her for a few minutes—the family have been delayed, it's been a great shock to them too. But Sister

Marton tells me you have a special relationship with Mrs Bateson?' His eyes were narrowed.

Colour flooded her cheeks. 'Er—yes, I—I like to think I do,' she nodded.

'Then I would appreciate it if you would continue to sit with her once I've left.'

'Yes, Doc—er—sir. Of course.' She felt no hesitation, although they both knew she should have been off duty hours ago. Or perhaps he didn't know; he was hardly likely to know the hours of a first-year nurse. But it didn't matter anyway, she had no intention of leaving the elderly lady.

Marcus Hamilton nodded dismissively. 'Get yourself a cup of tea and something to eat while I'm with Mrs Bateson. You have about ten minutes,' he told her arrogantly.

Miraculously Sister Marton had arranged a hot meal and drink for her. 'You should have gone hours ago,' she tutted as she supervised the meal. 'But Mr Hamilton has been most insistent that you stay with Mrs Bateson. I must say that in the circumstances, I agree with him.'

The consultant strode from the ward exactly ten minutes later, his jaw rigid as Olivia hurried past him to return to the elderly lady's bedside.

'He's a nice young man,' Mrs Bateson sighed, 'but he doesn't understand a love like Bert's and mine.'

'He's married——'

'Separated, he told me.' She shook her head. 'You young people take your marriage vows so lightly nowadays!'

'I'm not married, Mrs Bateson,' Olivia reminded her gently.

'You will be.' Mrs Bateson nodded approvingly. 'And your husband is going to be a lucky man. You're a lovely child, Olivia, so wait for the right man to come along—like I did.'

Shortly after that the elderly lady fell asleep, although Olivia still remained at her side, the gnarled work-worn fingers curved trustingly about hers. It had been dark for several hours when Marcus Hamilton appeared again, and considering what a busy man he was Olivia was touched by his concern for his patient. It couldn't have been the most pleasant of duties to tell her about her husband.

Olivia easily released her hand this time, making her way outside the curtains to speak to him.

'How is she?' His expression was grim.

'Asleep,' she whispered, as the rest of the ward settled down for the night. 'Where are her family?'

'The daughter who was coming to sit with her mother collapsed in Emergency,' he frowned. 'Quite understandable. But unfortunately we didn't make the connection between them until a few minutes ago. I've just come to check Mrs Bateson before letting her in to see her mother.' He went in to see his patient.

He was gone for several minutes, a hand to his temple as he left the bedside. 'You may as well go, Nurse King,' he told her curtly. 'There's nothing more you can do here.'

Olivia pushed past him, not caring in that moment who or what he was, her panicked gaze fixed on the still figure of Mrs Bateson. 'I—You—She isn't dead,' she choked. 'She can't be!'

'She is.' His hands steadied her as she would have swayed and fallen. 'About an hour ago, I would say. She just seems to have stopped breathing.'

'No!'

'Nurse King——'

'Leave me alone!' She wrenched out of his arms and ran from the ward, the tears falling unchecked.

She ran from the building and into the grounds, stumbling her way through the built-up garden towards the nurses' home, unaware that she had been followed until strong arms stopped her progress, swinging her round so that she found her face buried against a hard chest.

'I'm sorry,' Marcus Hamilton murmured, letting her cry for several minutes into his snowy white shirt, smelling slightly of some tangy aftershave. 'That's enough, Olivia!' He finally shook her gently as she couldn't seem to stop the tears.

She raised a tear-wet face to him. 'It doesn't seem fair. She was so nice—they both were.'

He produced a snowy white handkerchief and gently began to dry her cheeks. 'You haven't looked at this from her point of view, you know,' he said softly, concentrating on his task.

Olivia swallowed hard, standing docilely in front of him now. 'I don't understand . . .'

'She's with her husband now, the way she wanted to be.'

'Do you really believe that?'

He nodded. 'Of course. So it isn't a time to cry, is it?'

'I——'

'She would never have got well again, Olivia,' he told her gently. 'We'd done all we could for her—and it just wasn't enough.'

She bit her lip. 'It still doesn't seem fair.'

'Life seldom is.' He held out his handkerchief to her. 'Blow your nose,' he encouraged softly. 'You'll feel better.'

'I—I have my own.' Now that the shock was passing she was beginning to realise how unorthodox this was. Marcus Hamilton shouldn't even know she was alive, let alone be comforting her like this! 'I'm sorry,' she sounded more controlled now, 'I—I didn't mean to cry all over you.'

'You've just never been that close to death before?' he prompted.

'No,' she confirmed huskily.

'Believe me,' his voice was gruff as he straightened his shoulders wearily, 'it never gets any easier.'

Olivia blinked up at him in surprise, her lashes still spiky and damp from where she had been crying. Marcus Hamilton was very pale, a ring of white tension about his mouth, his expression strained. 'I'm sorry,' she said dazedly, 'I didn't realise.'

'People seldom do,' he rasped. 'Doctors aren't supposed to feel emotions, especially surgeons.'

'I really am sorry.' It had never occurred to her that this hard man could be affected by death as much as she was.

'But you still aren't convinced, are you?' he said ruefully.

'Convinced?' She looked puzzled, sure that if he said he was upset by Mrs Bateson's death then he was. What reason would he have to lie?

'That I can feel as much as the next man,' he drawled in reply.

'Oh, I—But I——' her words were cut off by a coolly possessive mouth claiming hers. Marcus Hamilton was kissing her! It seemed hard to believe, although the ruthless insistence of his lips couldn't be imagined. 'Mr Hamilton!' she gasped when he at last raised his head to look down at her.

'Indeed,' he derided. 'Shocking, isn't it?'

'Well, I—I wouldn't go so far as to say that,' she blushed.

'Wouldn't you?' Dark brows rose over steely grey eyes.

'No,' she admitted shyly. She had liked the way he kissed her, not been shocked by it. Surprised would be a better way of describing the way she felt. He was so experienced, had kissed her with a thoroughness that set her heart racing, his lips evoking a response from her that had been as spontaneous as it was unreserved.

'I would.' He put her firmly away from him, his expression grim. 'I have a daughter only six years younger than you.'

'And I have a father fifteen years older than you,' she retorted. 'So please don't try to make it look as if you're in the least like a father-figure to me.'

Humour lightened the colour of his eyes. 'That's put me firmly in my place! Thank you, Olivia,' he said soberly. 'I think I occasionally need reminding that thirty-three isn't old. Now off you go. And please believe that Mrs Bateson is where she wanted to be—with her husband.'

'Yes,' she nodded. 'And thank you—for everything.'

'My pleasure,' he drawled derisively before turning back towards the hospital building.

Olivia absently answered the greetings she received on the way to her room. She still grieved for Mrs Bateson, would miss her smiling cheerfulness on the ward, and this loss pushed the importance of that unexpected kiss from her mind.

She only had one more day to work before four straight days off, the two days of this week joining up with the two for next week, giving her a nice long break. But that one day on the ward seemed to drag by, the empty bed in the middle of the room a constant reminder of Mrs Bateson's death. Her fully recovered daughter came on to the ward late that afternoon to collect her mother's things, and her red-rimmed eyes told the whole story of how heartbroken she was to lose both her parents on the same day.

Olivia's days off were welcome after the trauma and strain of that last day, although as usual she spent the time at the nurses' home, only very rarely making the journey from this London hospital to her parents' home in Wales.

On the third day she attended the joint funeral of the Batesons. She had never been to a funeral before, and wasn't particularly looking forward to going to this one, and yet her genuine affection for the elderly couple merited this last show of respect on her behalf.

She didn't wear black, not being a member of the family, but her clothing was sombre, the brightness of her shoulder-length hair muted by being secured at her nape with a black ribbon.

The buses ran regularly from outside the hospital, and she could see the right one coming for her destination as she reached the bus stop?

'Like a lift, Olivia?'

She frowned down at the driver of the huge car parked at the side of the road. 'Mr Hamilton . . .'

He leant over to thrust the passenger door open. 'Get in.'

'Oh, but——'

'I'm going to the funeral too, Olivia,' he told her abruptly. 'Please get in,' he repeated. 'I'm about to cause a traffic jam.' He looked pointedly at the rapidly approaching bus.

She climbed into the burgundy-coloured Rolls-Royce, the engine only a gentle purr in the background as they drove further into town.

'You look different out of uniform,' Marcus Hamilton suddenly broke the tense silence between them. At least, it was tense on Olivia's part, as usual she could tell nothing of this man's feelings, from his enigmatic expression.

'Thank you—I think,' she added uncertainly.

For the first time since she had seen him he smiled, deep grooves visible in his cheeks, his teeth very white against his dark skin, his eyes a warm grey. 'You can take it as a compliment,' he drawled. 'Although the uniform is quite flattering on you too.'

She blushed shyly. She hadn't seen him the last three days except for a brief glimpse on the ward on

Friday, and remembering that kiss they had shared she felt embarrassed about being with him now.

'We're going to a funeral, Olivia,' he derided at her silence. 'Not to my home.'

'Yes—er—sir.'

'Marcus,' he substituted hardly.

She couldn't possibly be that informal with this autocratic man, so she remained silent for the remainder of the drive, swallowing hard as he parked the car with the others outside the church.

He studied her pale face as he helped her out of the car. 'It's all right, Olivia,' he assured her softly, clasping her elbow once again after locking the car. 'I'll be right beside you. If you want to come out just say so and we will.'

The service was short and beautiful, the words for the elderly couple sincerely moving, and the tears flowed unchecked. A snowy white handkerchief suddenly appeared in front of Olivia's blurred gaze, and she took it gratefully.

'This is getting to be a habit,' Marcus murmured softly. 'No, keep it,' he advised as she offered it back to him. 'You might need it again.'

She stood silently at his side as she spoke to the family outside after the service, his hand still firm on her elbow as he offered his quiet condolences.

'I'm afraid Olivia and I have to get back now,' he politely refused the eldest daughter's invitation back to the house.

'We realise what busy people you are,' the woman gave them a wan smile. 'We're just grateful you could come.'

Almost as if they were actually a couple! No one seemed to think it in the least odd that they were here together like this.

Well, Olivia thought it very odd. Senior consultants just didn't take this amount of interest in their juniors, and yet the masculine smell of cologne that clung to the handkerchief she still held told her it was all reality.

'Tea?' Marcus suggested on the drive back to the hospital.

'Er—no,' she answered awkwardly, 'thank you. I have to get back now.'

'Why?'

'Sorry?' she frowned.

'Why do you have to get back?' Marcus nodded. 'This is your day off, isn't it? Unless of course you have a date now?' he quirked one dark brow.

'How did you know it was my day off?'

'Well, you're here, aren't you?' he mocked.

She blushed at her stupidty. But however much she would have liked to have tea with him, to have perhaps learnt more about the break-up of his marriage, and his little girl, it just wasn't possible. Years of protocol established long before she was born dictated that she couldn't accept his invitation. She just wished she knew what had prompted him to make it.

'I do have a date,' she invented. 'Maybe some other time.'

'Yes,' his voice was terse. 'As you say, some other time.'

Olivia was aware of his silent anger for the rest of the journey, but what else had he expected! He might find it amusing to be entertained by her for a few hours, but she had to face the rest of the hospital staff, not him. The gossip about them wouldn't touch him in his lofty position, but she would come out of it less unscathed.

It wasn't until she reached her room in the nurses' home that she remembered his handkerchief still clutched in her hand. She would have to launder it and return it to him as soon as possible. And if she were honest with herself she was pleased to have this excuse to talk to him again.

Her opportunity came her first day back at work. Marcus was doing his usual ward round, with six or seven student doctors hanging on his every word and Sister Marton hovering on the edge of the crowd seeing that he had each patient's notes at the precise moment he needed them. Marcus was the first to leave Sister Marton's office after the round, so Olivia seized her opportunity.

'Mr Hamilton!' She hurried after him, pulling the neatly folded handkerchief out of her pocket.

He took it wordlessly, pushing it into his breast pocket; several files were tucked under his other arm.

She touched the sleeve of his jacket. 'I—Thank you.'

'Yes.' He looked down pointedly at her hand, meeting her gaze coolly after she had removed it. 'If you'll excuse me . . .'

She took the rebuff for exactly what it was, making a promise to herself that she wouldn't bother him again. He obviously regretted his friendliness of yesterday, and she wouldn't remind him of it again!

She might have decided that, but it didn't stop her feeling any less miserable, and the news that she had a telephone call later that evening didn't help either. Her steps were slow as she went to the communal callbox in the nurses' home.

She knew who it was going to be, knew there would probably be another argument with her mother because she didn't go home enough. Never mind the fact that she and her father argued non-stop when she did go home!

'Hello,' she greeted lightly, deciding she might as well start off on the right foot!

The voice that answered her was definitely male, and it wasn't her father. 'Olivia?'

'Yes,' she frowned her uncertainty, not recognising the voice at all.

'I'd like to see you. I *have* to see you,' the man amended raggedly.

'Who is that?' she demanded to know.

'God, I must be mad,' he muttered to himself. 'I'm sorry I troubled you. I——'

'Marcus!' she suddenly realised. 'Marcus, is that you?'

'Yes,' he confirmed shakily. 'I've just had a scene with Sally, and I——'

'Sally?'

'My daughter,' he explained impatiently. 'It doesn't matter, I shouldn't have called you. I'm sorry I bothered you.'

'Would you like to talk about it?' she prompted gently, ignoring his lapse back into the controlled consultant, appealing to the man who had telephoned her out of desperation.

There was silence for several long seconds after her question. 'Yes,' he sighed at last. 'I have to talk to someone. But it's so difficult over the telephone, and I can't leave Sally, it's our housekeeper's night off.'

'Where do you live?' she asked.

'Where do I——? Olivia, are you saying you'll come here?' He sounded astounded.

'If you want me to,' she answered without hesitation, no longer caring that he was a top consultant and she was only a junior nurse; they were a man and a woman, and Marcus needed to be with someone tonight. She felt grateful that she was that someone, felt a new maturity at his trust in her.

'Olivia, are you sure this is what you want?' He seemed to hesitate.

'As sure as you were when you decided to make the call,' she told him briskly. 'The address?'

He didn't hesitate any more—and neither did she, grabbing a lightweight jacket to pull on over her blouse, the latter tucked into her denims, her waist, narrow hips and long legs all clearly outlined against the skin-tight material. The taxi-driver raised his brows as she gave him the address, charging her an exorbitant fee, since the address indicated she could well afford it, being in a quietly exclusive part of London, the house one of several in a private square.

Marcus opened the door before she even had time to ring the bell, looking completely different from the Marcus Hamilton she had come to know as he walked about the hospital, as casually dressed as herself, in black trousers and a grey shirt unbuttoned partway down his throat. His avid gaze searched her shy face. 'Olivia . . .!' he breathed.

'Yes,' she said needlessly.

He gave a ragged sigh, pulling her inside the house before taking her hungrily into his arms. '*God*, Olivia!' His mouth came down fiercely on hers, bending her body into his as she clung to him, making no secret of his desire for her. 'Olivia, Olivia, *Olivia*!' He smoothed back her tumbled curls, the last cry of her name coming out as a triumphant laugh, one of his rare smiles lighting his austere features. 'God, you're beautiful!' He shook his head almost dazedly.

She moistened her lips, aware that they had a tingling sensation from the force of his kiss. 'I am?' She gave an uncertain smile.

'You are.' With his arm still about her waist he took her into the lounge, a strange uncomfortably modern room, the furniture all angles and squares, white fluffy rugs scattered about the highly polished floor, modern pictures hung on the white walls. It didn't look like Marcus at all. 'My wife's choice of décor,' he explained with feeling. 'I just haven't got around to changing it yet.'

'Of course,' she bit on her bottom lip. 'You're separated.'

He nodded abruptly and moved away from her. 'In

the process of getting a divorce. Which is precisely the reason Sally and I argued.'

'Oh,' Olivia grimaced. 'Do you think it's wise to argue with her about it? She needs your love and understanding, not more arguments.'

He sighed. 'I've tried to be understanding, but I'm afraid it isn't a two-way thing at the moment. Sally has the ridiculous idea that I'm going to start bringing a string of different women to the house.' He saw her smile, his expression rueful as he thrust his hands into his trouser pockets. 'I know—hardly my image, is it?'

'Daddy——' A young girl came to a halt in the doorway, her rebellious grey eyes focusing on Olivia before she turned angrily on her father. 'You didn't waste any time, did you?' she accused. 'And to think I came down here to apologise for being silly!'

'Sally——'

'Leave me alone!' she almost spat the words at him. 'Mummy was right, men aren't to be trusted!' She slammed back out of the room.

Stunned silence followed her exit before Olivia hastily gathered her thoughts together. 'I don't think it was such a good idea for me to come here after all. I thought if you could talk to me I might be able to help, but instead I've——'

'Been subjected to my daughter's rudeness,' Marcus said grimly, running a weary hand through the dark thickness of his hair. 'It's been like this ever since Ruth and I separated six months ago. I'm running out of solutions.'

'I think all your daughter needs is time—and me out of the house,' Olivia added ruefully. 'I think you should go up and talk to her.'

'And what are you going to do?' He looked at her with narrowed eyes.

She shrugged. 'I'll go back to the nursing home and do some studying—and goodness knows I need to!'

she added lightly. 'I don't know how you ever remember it all.'

'Experience,' he derided dryly. 'You really do want to go?'

'I think I should,' she answered evasively.

'But do you want to?' He watched her intently.

'No,' she admitted truthfully.

'I was hoping that would be your answer,' he gave another of his rare but mesmerising smiles. 'My housekeeper usually sits with Sally if I'm out in the evening, so will you have dinner with me tomorrow evening?' His hands grasped her upper arms strongly.

Olivia was almost hypnotised by the deep grey of his eyes. 'Yes,' she said breathlessly. 'Yes, I'd like to.'

It was to be the first of many evenings they were to spend together, although on none of them was Marcus ever as intense as he had been that first evening at his home. He would be an entertaining companion, give her a chaste kiss on the cheek before they parted, usually arranging to see her again in a couple of days' time, but never again did he kiss her with passion.

By tacit agreement they didn't make their friendship obvious at the hospital, being completely cool to each other whenever they happened to meet there. And although several of Olivia's friends teased her about her mysterious new boy-friend, none of them guessed she was secretly seeing Marcus Hamilton. She wasn't sure any of them would have believed her if she had told them—she wasn't sure she believed it herself half the time!

Sally Hamilton had point-blankly refused to meet her, and in the circumstances Olivia couldn't exactly blame her. She wasn't even sure herself what part she played in Marcus's life; she only knew that for the moment he seemed to need her, her quiet presence, her gentle teasing if he should happen to become too grim. And not once did he mention his wife to her, whether through marital bitterness or just uninterest, she didn't know.

Then one night their relationship changed drastically, Marcus telephoning her urgently to put off their meeting for that evening. 'My mother-in-law has turned up to see Sally,' he explained tersely. 'I can hardly deny her, she is Sally's grandmother.'

'Of course,' Olivia agreed quietly, for the first time realising the consequences of going out with a man who was still married to another woman. 'I understand,' she said, not understanding at all. Was Marcus ashamed of his relationship with her, was that why he was so determined no one should know about it?

There was silence at the other end of the telephone for several long minutes as Marcus sensed her confusion. 'Come and meet Sybil,' he invited suddenly. 'Then you'll see why I was so anxious for you not to do so.'

She did indeed. Sybil Carr was still a beautiful woman despite being in her mid-fifties, her figure slender, her black hair fashionable grey at the peak. She was also bitchy and condescending, treating Olivia as being no older than her granddaughter, the latter having graciously consented to sit down to dinner with Olivia, obviously enjoying her grandmother's treatment of the woman she didn't like and had no intention of attempting to like.

It was a strained and uncomfortable evening for Olivia, and Sybil Carr's friendly word of warning about 'middle-aged men trying to recapture their youth with a younger woman' was the worst of it. The two women unexpectedly found themselves alone in the lounge when Marcus went upstairs to say goodnight to Sally, and Sybil Carr took full advantage of the opportunity this gave her to warn Olivia off him.

'Well?' Marcus arched dark brows questioningly as he drove her back to the nurses' home.

'I shouldn't have come,' she confirmed woodenly, still shaken by what Sybil Carr had said to her. 'Your mother-in-law believes you will eventually go back to your wife.' The words came out in a rush as she couldn't hold them in any longer.

He stiffened, his expression remote. 'I wasn't the one to leave, she was.'

'And if she wanted to come back?'

'She's never asked to.'

'But——'

'I do not wish to discuss my wife, Olivia,' he told her harshly. 'She has no relevance to our relationship. Sybil may believe what she likes, but I don't expect you to listen to her.'

If only she had more confidence in his feelings for her! And yet Sybil Carr had been so patronising about Marcus's interest in her, had called it a fantasy for him, every man's dream of having a young girl infatuated with him. She had also pointed out that Marcus needed someone with more sophistication, that he would soon tire of a child like her. Her last warning had had the most effect on Olivia, telling her that Ruth Hamilton had realised the mistake she made in leaving her husband and daughter, that she was now prepared to come home.

Marcus hadn't denied wanting his wife back, now, he had merely said she hadn't asked to come back. There was a vast difference between the two answers.

'Olivia?'

'Sorry.' She came out of her reverie to look at him, finding his gaze levelled on her. 'Your mother-in-law doesn't like me.'

His expression lightened as he turned back to the road. 'She isn't supposed to, *I* am.'

'And do you?' she asked huskily.

His hand left the steering-wheel to grasp hers. 'You know I do.'

'I—You never show me that you do,' she said hesitantly, needing his reassurance tonight. 'You're always so—distant with me.'

He didn't answer her, taking his hand from hers to stare rigidly ahead. Heavens, what had she done now!

Marcus stopped the car a short distance from the hosptial as he usually did, turning to look at her. 'Olivia——' he seemed to be searching for the right words. 'If I—I'm afraid that if I once start kissing you I won't be able to stop! Can you understand that?' He looked at her appealingly.

Her eyes were wide. 'No.'

He sighed. 'I didn't think you would. Come here.' He opened his arms to her.

She went into them unquestioningly, gasping at the fierceness with which he claimed her lips, moulding her torso to his, making her aware of the rapid beat of his heart. One hand moved to curve possessively over her breast, locating the taut nipple through the thin material of her blouse, his touch sure and demanding.

'I want you,' he groaned into her throat. 'I want you so, Olivia.'

She was lost in the wonder of his caresses after weeks of starvation, loving the feel of his lips against her skin, her head thrown back as he smoothed the material away from her breasts, capturing one red-tipped nipple between his pleasure-giving lips, his tongue erotic against the hardened nub, and spasms of pleasure coursed through her body. She held his head against her, her fingers fevered in the thickness of his hair, kissing his temple with trembling lips, gasping as his teeth bit gently into her sensitive nipple, causing no pain, only pleasure.

'Come home with me. Olivia,' he murmured against her mouth, nibbling gently on the lower lip, drawing it into his own in a message of eroticism. 'Come home and share my bed,' he encouraged raggedly.

'I——'

'Olivia? Olivia, telephone!'

Her memories of Marcus were interrupted with a suddenness that left her stunned for several seconds. It had all seemed so vivid, so real, just as if it had happened yesterday and not six years ago.

'Olivia?' A brief knock was followed by Natalie actually coming into the bedroom. 'There's a telephone call for you.'

Olivia dragged herself back from the past with effort, standing up. 'Do you know who it is?' She pushed her hair back from her face.

'Sally Hamilton,' Natalie supplied in a puzzled voice. 'And she sounded very urgent.'

Olivia froze as soon as she heard the name of her caller. What on earth could Sally Hamilton want to talk to her about? The girl had seemed pleased to see her this afternoon, and it had been nice to see what a pleasant young woman she had grown up into. But Olivia didn't want the meeting to go any further than that, and she intended making that clear to Sally.

She picked up the receiver as it lay beside the telephone in the hallway, conscious of Natalie's curious looks before she went back to join the family in the lounge. 'Sally, I——'

'Oh, thank God you're there!' the girl choked before Olivia could say any more. 'It's Daddy, he—he's been in a serious car accident. He—he has head injuries. Olivia, they aren't sure if—if he's going to live!'

CHAPTER TWO

'OLIVIA! Olivia, are you still there?'

'I—Yes,' she answered dully. 'I—Did you say your father has been injured?' She spoke so calmly, in such a controlled voice, almost as if this were all a bad dream and Sally hadn't just told her Marcus had been seriously hurt.

'He crashed into a truck.' Sally was crying quietly now. 'He was called out to an emergency at the hospital, and he—he crashed on his way back.'

'I see.' Olivia's emotions were numb.

'Will you come to the hospital?'

The suggestion shocked her out of her emotionless voice. Go and see Marcus? She couldn't do that! 'No——'

'I need you, Olivia,' Sally sobbed.

'Your grandmother——' she began.

'Has completely gone to pieces. It isn't long since Grandfather died, and this accident on top of that . . . She's been sedated. I need to be with someone who loves him as much as I do——'

'I don't love your father, Sally,' Olivia interrupted sharply.

'But you did once, you admitted as much earlier today. Oh, Olivia, please!'

'I can't, Sally. You know I can't,' she said in a distressed voice, her hand tight around the receiver.

'I thought you cared,' Sally choked accusingly. 'I really thought you cared!' The receiver was put down with a loud clatter.

Olivia sank ino the chair next to the telephone, staring sightlessly at the wall opposite. She *couldn't* go

39

to the hospital. What would be the point? Marcus would no more want her there than she wanted to see him. But Sally said he might not even live! Marcus dead? No, she couldn't even begin to accept that.

Sally's desolation came back to haunt her too. She was such a child still, and her father was all she had. Olivia couldn't let her go through this alone.

'Olivia!' Natalie exclaimed in a shocked voice as she came out of the lounge and saw her pale face, coming down on her haunches in front of her. 'What is it? What's wrong?'

She moistened her numbed lips. 'Sally's father has—he's been in an accident,' she explained dully. 'She wants me to go to the hospital and sit with her.'

Natalie frowned. 'I see—I think.'

Delicate colour darkened Olivia's pale cheeks. 'I knew Mr Hamilton years ago,' she explained.

'I sensed something this afternoon——'

'We worked at the same hospital, that's all,' Olivia insisted sharply.

Natalie squeezed her hand as if she understood. 'I'll tell the family that you've had to go and see a friend who's in hospital,' she said gently.

'Thank you,' she accepted gratefully, going up the stairs to get her car keys.

'I hope he's all right,' Natalie encouraged softly as Olivia came back down the stairs. 'I've met him a couple of times, he's a nice man.'

Olivia didn't answer her, not at all sure that she had ever thought Marcus a 'nice' man herself. She had been deeply attracted to him, but that hadn't stopped her knowing of the coldness about him. But even though she hadn't seen him for six years the thought of him dying still filled her with horror. She had been young, had loved him with an innocence that couldn't help but be hurt by such a coolly contained man.

She wasn't familiar with the hospital he had been

taken to, and it took her several extra minutes to locate it, several more minutes to ascertain that Mr Hamilton was still in the examination room and that his daughter was in the waiting-room.

Sally was a forlorn figure sitting alone in the corner of the room, but she looked up hopefully as the door opened, bursting into loud relieved sobs as she ran across the room into Olivia's arms.

'It's all right,' she soothed the girl softly. 'It's all right, Sally.'

'I knew you'd come!' Sally clung to her. 'I just knew you wouldn't let me down!'

Then she had known a lot more than Olivia did! Even as she parked the car outside in the hospital car park she had been having second thoughts as to the sensibility of this visit. There was always the possiblity that Marcus might not remember her—after all, she had meant little in his life, but then again if he did remember her, seeing her again could upset him. And if he was as ill as Sally said he was then that wasn't going to help him at all. She also had to admit, to herself at least, that not all her concern was for Marcus's sake; she had no idea how she was going to feel about seeing him again after all this time.

'Has there been any more news?' she prompted gently.

Sally shook her head, blowing her nose noisily before wiping her tear-stained cheeks. 'None. I've been sitting here for hours—well, almost two,' she amended. 'It just seems longer. And I haven't seen the doctor since I signed the form for Daddy to go into surgery.'

'You mean Mar—he's being operated on right now?' Olivia gasped.

'Yes,' the girl confirmed huskily. 'He has a fractured skull.'

'Dear God . . .!' Olivia groaned, pulling herself

together as she suddenly realised she couldn't be helping Sally at all by reacting like this. 'He'll be all right,' she assured her softly. 'I'll go and see if I can find out anything new. You sit here and I'll bring you back a cup of coffee.'

'You won't be long?' Sally clutched on to her hand, evidence of her fears of the last two hours.

Olivia smiled, squeezing the hand she held. 'No, I won't be long. And don't worry, I'm sure your father is going to be just fine.'

Her confidence lasted for as long as it took her to get out of the waiting-room. She knew the complications that could arise from a fractured skull as well as any other trained medical person. Thank God Sally didn't seem to be as well informed, otherwise she might be in a worse state than she was already.

She easily located the Sister on Emergency in her office, quickly explained who and what she was, and asked for further information on Marcus.

The pretty young Sister gave her a sympathetic look. 'We're all very concerned too. He's the Chief Surgeon here, you know.'

No, she hadn't known that! 'Then who is operating . . .?'

'Mr Hamilton's condition was critical when he was brought in,' the other girl sighed heavily. 'Mr Hamilton's own assistant, Simon Brooks, is operating.' She shook her head. 'I feel partly responsible for the accident.'

Olivia frowned. '*You* do?' What did this girl mean to Marcus? She was certainly young and pretty enough for him to find attractive.

'If I hadn't called him out for an emergency operation he wouldn't have been in this part of London at all,' the Sister explained.

Olivia heaved a mental sigh of relief—although why she should she had no idea. Marcus Hamilton was just an excellent surgeon to her now, nothing more. She didn't care if he had a dozen women in his life. Now she *was* starting to sound jealous!

'I'll just go along to the theatre and check for you,' the young Sister told her. 'I won't be long.'

'I'll be in the waiting-room with Sally—Mr Hamilton's daughter,' Olivia explained in case the other woman didn't know her.

She took the promised coffee back to Sally, heavily sugared, although she saw Sally grimace as she tasted the sweetness but bravely drink it down anyway, knowing that it would be good for her.

The Sister came in about ten minutes later. 'Mr Hamilton is just coming out of Theatre now,' she informed them gently.

'And?' Olivia prompted, white with anxiety.

'He's no longer on the danger list——'

'Oh, thank God!' Sally collapsed into Olivia's waiting arms.

But Olivia knew the Sister hadn't finished, could see by the compassion in the deep blue eyes that there was more to come. She tensed herself for that.

'Mr Brooks removed several fragments of bone that had fractured,' the other woman continued softly. 'We have no idea yet what damage may have been done internally.'

'You mean—you mean brain damage?' Sally gasped.

'It's a possibility——'

It was what Olivia had been expecting, and she felt Sally sag against her as she fainted.

'I'm so sorry,' the Sister helped her to get Sally into a chair, 'but Mr Brooks is in with another emergency right now, and I don't believe Miss Hamilton should be under any delusions as to how serious her father's injuries are.'

'She had to be told,' Olivia assured her.

'Mr Hamilton is being moved to a private room

now, there will be a nurse in with him, but I'm sure Mr Brooks will have no objection to both you and Miss Hamilton sitting with him if you want to.'

Looking at Sally, Olivia knew the young girl would want to, and she couldn't let her do it alone.

'Mr Brooks will be in to talk to you both as soon as he's available,' the Sister told her. 'In the meantime——' she hesitated, 'Mr Hamilton also had severe lacerations to the face. You understand?'

A shiver ran down Olivia's spine. Marcus's beautiful handsome face cut and torn, possibly scarred for life? If he had a life . . .! God, he must be all right, he *must*!

'I'll prepare her,' she told the other girl softly as Sally began to regain consciousness, groaning groggily as she did so.

But no one had prepared her! Marcus lay grey against the stark white bedclothes, a heavy bandage about his temple, several deep cuts on his face that had needed stitches, blood congealed along the jagged edges, the skin already looking bruised. There were several stitched cuts on his hands as they lay limply on the counterpane too, as if he had put up his hands to shield his face. Heaven knows what he would have looked like if he hadn't put up his hands!

Sally wordlessly pulled up a chair to sit at his side, gently touching one of his injured hands so as not to hurt him, her gaze never leaving his still face.

A nurse sat silently at the back of the room, so Olivia sat in the chair opposite Sally's across the bed, not touching Marcus herself, afraid even of that much contact with him. He hadn't changed at all in six years, perhaps a little harsher in the face, but other than that he looked the same, the lines grooved beside his nose and mouth smoothed out in his unconscious state. His breathing was shallow and even, hardly breathing at all really.

'I won't let him die.' Sally suddenly broke the

silence, speaking with a calm that had Olivia looking at
her with sharp concern.

'Sally——'

'I won't let him be a mental cabbage either,' the
young girl told her fiercely.

Olivia gasped, not having acknowledged such a
thing even to herself. That could never happen to
Marcus, not with his gift for healing others, a skill that
would need every ounce of his old sure intelligence if
he were to continue with it.

'I won't!' Sally repeated vehemently.

Olivia wisely remained silent, not wanting to say or do
anything that would push the emotional tension Sally
was under over the edge, knowing the younger girl was
likely to collapse altogether when that happened.

They sat there for what seemed like hours, although
Olivia knew that in fact only two hours had passed
since they were shown into Marcus's room. She took
advantage of one of the occasions she went out to the
machine to get coffee to call the Hayes house and
assure them that so far Marcus was holding his own.
For once Clara hadn't seemed so vague, telling her
that of course she must stay at the hospital with Sally
for as long as she needed her.

When she got back to the room it was to find Sally
slumped back in her chair, fast asleep. She didn't even
bother to move the girl into a more comfortable
position, not wanting to disturb her, knowing that
sleep was the best thing for her right now. She would
need all of her strength when Marcus finally woke up.

Dear God, seeing him like this, near enough to
touch, took her back once more to that night he had
asked her to share his bed.

'Your mother-in-law,' she had reminded him
protestingly.

'Sybil isn't staying at the house. She'll probably
have left by now,' he told her.

'But——'

'I want to make love to you, Olivia,' Marcus had stated calmly. 'And I think you want it too.'

'Yes . . .' She made no effort to deny the yearning ache he had evoked.

'Then you'll come home with me?' he persisted intensely.

'No,' she refused shakily. 'I—I can't.'

He sat back with a groan, his head back on the head-rest, his eyes closed. 'I'm too old to play games, Olivia,' he told her harshly. 'I warned you that once I started kissing you I wouldn't want to stop. I can't go back to our sterile relationship, not now, not when I've seen you, touched you.'

She swallowed hard. 'Are you saying that if I don't go home with you now you won't see me again?'

'I don't know what I'm saying!' He ran an agitated hand through his already tousled hair. 'I can't think straight right now.' He took her hand in his, guiding it down his body. 'Feel how badly I want you,' he rasped.

'Oh, Marcus . . .!' she began to tremble.

'Yes,' he thrust her hand away. 'And I feel like this most of the time. Up until now, until you asked me to show you how I felt about you, I've been in control of the situation. I know how very young you are, how inexperienced, and I've kept my distance because of that. But after tonight I can't do that. Do you understand what I'm saying now?'

'Yes.'

'Go in now, Olivia,' he instructed harshly. 'We'll talk again tomorrow.

'Marcus——'

'Yes?'

His abrupt tone chilled her, her agreement to do what he wanted, go where he wanted suddenly not seeming like a good idea after all. 'Nothing,' she bit her lip. 'I'll see you tomorrow.'

'Yes.' He didn't even turn as she got out of the car.

Olivia looked down now at the man who lay so still and white in the hospital bed beside her, amazed that he could have caused such havoc in her life. Of course, she had been too young to cope with all that he wanted from her, but that hadn't stopped her wanting to *be* all he needed. In the end it had nearly destroyed her.

He began to move restlessly in the bed, to groan in his unconscious state, his lips moving soundlessly as he fought against the covers that confined him.

'You're all right, Marcus,' she told him softly, knowing he was nowhere near regaining consciousness yet, but wanting to reassure him anyway. 'We're here, Sally and Olivia.'

'Olivia,' he muttered, startling her with the ferocity of his tone. 'God, Ruth! She means nothing to me. Olivia. No, don't go, it's you I love.' He muttered unintelligibly for several seconds. 'No, don't leave me,' he groaned. 'Ruth. She means nothing to me. Olivia, nothing. God, I love you, I love you. Please don't go, not again. Ruth ...' he trailed off into oblivion once more.

The tears were streaming down Olivia's face by the time he had finished, and she moved away as the nurse came forward to check on him. Even in his unconscious state Marcus still hadn't forgotten his love for his wife. It had been because of that love that he and Olivia had finally parted.

Instead of the two of them talking the next day as Marcus had said they would, he cancelled their date for that evening. Olivia didn't even bother to ask him why, she could guess the reason, and knew he was finishing with her as gently as he knew how.

As she was coming off duty the next day she saw Marcus's car parked outside the main entrance of the hospital, and seated in the passenger seat was a

beautiful blonde woman of about thirty, her resem-
blance to Sally unmistakable. She knew immediately
that it was Ruth Hamilton, and as Sybil Carr had
predicted, Marcus had taken his wife back into his life.

At that moment he had come out of the hospital, not
noticing her as he got in the car beside his wife, giving
a smiling response to something his wife said to him as
they drove away.

In that moment Olivia had wanted to die, to run
away and hide. And then sanity had returned. Maybe
the situation wasn't quite as it looked, maybe Marcus
deserved the benefit of one telephone call just to be
sure. And she knew that she would have to talk to him
over the telephone if at all, knew she couldn't bear for
him to see her if he said it was all over between them.

She left making the call until she knew Marcus
should be at home, feeling dismay when Sybil Carr
answered the telephone.

'Marcus is upstairs, with Ruth,' the other woman
answered her request to speak to him. 'They're getting
ready to go out for the evening.'

'I see,' Olivia quivered. 'Could I—talk to him?'

'Well, I'm not sure that would be a good idea in the
circumstances, my dear,' the other woman mocked
lightly. 'Of course, he has told Ruth about you, and
I don't think she would appreciate your calling him
now. I gather Marcus hasn't spoken to you himself?'

Olivia swallowed hard, feeling utterly humiliated.
'No.'

'Naughty man,' Sybil laughed. 'Well, I'm happy to
say that Ruth and Marcus have decided to forgive each
other and start afresh. My daughter came back last night.'

Last night, when Marcus had cancelled their own
meeting so abruptly. It had to be true, Marcus had
been reconciled with his wife, had cruelly dismissed *her*
from his life as if he had never kissed her with such
passion, never asked her to share his bed.

'I'm sure Marcus means to tell you himself,' Sybil Carr continued. 'In fact, here he comes now. Shall I——'

'No!' Olivia refused sharply. 'Please don't trouble him. I—It wasn't important anyway.'

'Very well, my dear. If you're sure . . .?'

'Yes,' she confirmed abruptly.

'I'll tell him you called,' the other woman said kindly.

Whether she did or not, Olivia didn't hear from Marcus, and then two days later Marcus had asked for a leave of absence for 'family reasons'. Olivia knew exactly what those family reasons were too, she had seen just how beautiful Ruth Hamilton was, knew that Marcus would want to spend time alone with his wife for the new start to his marriage. Her own request for a transfer to another hospital had been dealt with so efficiently that by the time Marcus returned to work she had already gone.

For months she had lived in the hope of his reconciliation with Ruth not working out, selfishly wishing he would come looking for her to take her out again. She hadn't set eyes on him again until this moment.

And what a way for them to meet again, with Marcus seriously ill! He looked so weak just lying there, so helpless, and she had never seen Marcus helpless before. If—*when* he regained consciousness; she mentally reprimanded herself for even thinking in the negative, of course he would regain consciousness. And when he did he was going to resent his weakness and anyone who had seen him like this.

Looking down at him now she knew that her love for him all those years ago had been all the more intense because he had been her first real love. Perhaps if she hadn't been so young she could have coped with it all so much more easily, but as it was she had continued to think of him for the last six years, had compared every man she met to him—and always found them wanting. But Marcus was only a mere man after all, not the demi-god she had blown him up to be in her mind.

'Sally?' One of his hands suddenly moved gropingly across the bedclothes.

'She's here,' Olivia assured him, nodding to the nurse to go and get the doctor.

He turned in the half-light as he heard the door close behind the nurse, his eyes the same smoky grey Olivia remembered as he looked at her. 'Who are you?' he asked sharply, his voice exactly as she remembered it too, deep and throaty.

She moistened her suddenly dry lips, her thoughts of a few minutes ago now seeming superfluous when faced with the vibrantly alive man, her senses leaping just at the sound of his voice. 'My name is Olivia,' she told him softly.

'Olivia . . .' His attention seemed to wander for a few seconds, then he blinked still sleepy eyes. 'Why are you sitting here in the dark?'

'I——' she frowned, looking into his eyes once again, fear clutching at her heart. 'Does it seem very dark to you, Marcus?' She tried to keep her voice calm, although she wasn't sure she had succeeded. And where was the doctor, he should have been here by now!

Marcus moistened stiff lips, seeming to have trouble speaking. 'Very dark,' he nodded. 'Why don't you put the light on so that I can see you?'

Olivia began to shake, unable to stop the trembling of her hand as it moved to clasp his, unable to comprehend what he seemed to be telling her, finding speech impossible as she sought to comfort him. Where was that doctor!

'My God!' The panic screaming inside her suddenly

seemed to transmit itself to him as he attempted to sit up, somehow finding the strength to struggle against her restraining hands.

'Please, Marcus,' she begged, trying to calm him. 'You must lie down, you could make things worse.'

'Worse?' he choked. 'How can they be worse? I can't see,' he groaned. 'My God, I'm blind. I'm blind . . .!' The last came out in an agonised cry as he slumped back against the pillows in unconsciousness once again.

CHAPTER THREE

His shouting woke Sally, and when she saw the truth of his words in Olivia's stricken face, that those beautiful smoky grey eyes could see only darkness, she collapsed. The doctor at last hurried into the room, still dressed in the dark green clothes he had worn during surgery, checking on Marcus before carrying Sally out of the room.

'I think it might be better if you took Miss Hamilton home,' he told Olivia softly. 'Mr Hamilton should be out for another few hours now, so there's nothing she can do here.'

'But he's blind,' Olivia choked, the tears quietly falling. 'Marcus is blind!'

'I suspected as much,' he said dully; he was a young man in his early thrities, with kind brown eyes, fair hair, and a pleasantly handsome face. 'My name is Brooks, Miss King, Simon Brooks. I performed the operation on Mr Hamilton.'

'Yes,' she nodded, still too dazed to take in what was happening. 'How did your other emergency go?' It seemed ridiculous that she should even think of such a thing in her shock, but somehow the question just seemed to flow from her lips.

'Very well,' Simon Brooks patted her hand understandingly. 'You're a nurse, I believe?'

'Yes.'

'Then I don't have to tell you the seriousness of the operation I performed on Mr Hamilton. Those fragments of bone I removed were dangerously close to the optic nerve.'

Her eyes widened in horror. 'Then——'

52

'The damage—the blindness,' he amended with a ragged sigh, 'could be temporary—or it could be permanent. I have a specialist coming to see him tomorrow.'

Olivia felt sick. Marcus couldn't be blind! How could such a man lose his sight, never to know the sight of spring, the beauty of a summer's day, never be able to perform his wonderful operations again. It couldn't be true!

'I feel this as badly as you do, Miss King,' Simon Brooks said shakily. 'Marcus and I have worked together for over two years now. I respect him deeply as a surgeon, and I like him as a man. But I didn't have time to get in the specialist surgeon he needed, if I hadn't operated on him he would already be dead!' The doctor was too shaken to hide his stress; he was in need of comfort himself, the strain seeming to catch up with him.

'I understand.' And she did. A blind, alive Marcus was better than a dead one, although she didn't know if Marcus would feel the same way when he was finally conscious once again. Too many people believed, erroneously, that they had nothing to live for when left with such a disability, and Marcus was one of the proudest men she knew; he would hate the restrictions blindness would put on him.

'I just hope he will too,' the surgeon grimly echoed her thoughts.

'He will,' she squeezed his arm reassuringly. 'Now I'd better get Sally home.'

He frowned. 'Her grandmother collapsed too, I believe?'

'Yes,' she nodded.

'Then perhaps, as a family friend, you wouldn't mind staying with them tonight,' he suggested.

'Oh, but——'

'I don't think Miss Hamilton should be left on her own, and if her grandmother is sedated . . .'

Olivia could see she had no choice; she felt herself being drawn into a web of her own making, and she knew that by coming here tonight she had involved herself completely with the Hamilton family again. Anyone seeing her here with Sally tonight would, mistakenly, presume her to be a friend of the family, and it would look odd, not to mention callous, if she let Sally down now. But the thought of going to the Hamilton house didn't please her at all.

Sally was still in shock when she came round, and put up little resistance to Olivia's efforts to get her home, back to the house Marcus had occupied six years ago. His housekeeper was a very capable woman, who took in the situation at a glance, helping Olivia get Sally up to her bedroom and into bed, Olivia giving the young girl the injection Simon had instructed her to. Within minutes Sally had fallen into a drugged sleep, so Olivia quietly left the room.

'My God—you!' gasped a shocked voice behind her.

She turned sharply to confront Sybil Carr, a vastly changed Sybil, her face ravaged by grief, her body too thin, her hair in disarray. The other woman seemed to sway as she looked at her, and Olivia rushed to her side before she fell, helping her back into the bedroom she had just left.

'It is you, isn't it?' Sybil said dazedly as she was lowered back in to the bed.

'I'm Olivia King, yes,' Olivia replied briskly, making the other woman comfortable against the pillows.

'The girl Marcus—the one he was involved with all those years ago?' Sybil looked at her accusingly.

'Yes,' she confirmed tersely.

'But I don't understand. What are you doing here? Have you seen Marcus?' she demanded sharply.

'Yes, I've been sitting with him.'

'And is he—is he all right?'

In that moment she felt sorry for the older woman, even though she had been the one to tell Olivia her own dreams couldn't come true. The last six years had been more unkind to Sybil than to her; the older woman had lost her daughter, her husband, and now Marcus had been seriously injured. It was enough to throw anyone into hysteria, and Sally had gone through the same traumas. This last one involving Marcus could be one too many, for both of them.

'He regained consciousness briefly, and the doctor seemed satisfied with him,' she answered evasively. 'I think you should try and get some sleep now, Marcus is going to need you tomorrow.' She didn't feel up to coping with the other woman's possible hysterics right now, and maybe in the morning Sybil would be able to accept Marcus's blindness more calmly. If such a thing could ever be accepted calmly!

To her surprise she received no argument; the other woman looked as if she had every intention of sleeping as Olivia quietly left the room. The housekeeper met her downstairs, offering her a cup of tea.

'I'd prefer coffee,' she accepted gratefully, and went through to the lounge, unconsciously noting that the mellow golds and browns of the room were much more attractive than the stark white had been six years ago.

She drank more than one cup of coffee through the night, dozing in a chair, but all the time keeping half an ear alert to the sound of the telephone. Simon Brooks had promised he would call her if Marcus should wake up, and by the time Sally joined her at eight o'clock the next morning there had been no call from him.

'Grandmother won't be down this morning,' Sally told her quietly, very pale and drawn, dark hollows beneath her eyes. 'I—I've explained to her about Daddy.' She sat down abruptly.

Olivia bit her lip, knowing how hard it must have been for the girl to tell her grandmother such a thing. 'How did she take it?'

'Not very well, but she's calm now.' She leant her head back against the chair. 'You've been very kind, Olivia, I don't know how to thank you.'

'You don't have to,' she said huskily. 'I was glad to be able to help.'

'Did—did Daddy know you?'

Olivia had wondered that herself, but there hadn't seemed to be any recognition in the hard face. 'It's difficult to say,' she shrugged. 'But I don't think so.' She frowned as she saw the worried look on the other girl's face. 'He asked for you, Sally, so I don't think you need fear brain damage.'

'He's just blind,' Sally said bluntly, without emotion.

Olivia revised her first impression this morning of how well Sally was coping with her father's accident now that the first shock had worn off. The girl was too calm, too composed, and when the break came it could be like a dam bursting.

'He's alive, Sally,' she encouraged softly. 'That's the important thing.'

Sally stood up forcefully. 'I'm going back to the hospital, would you like to come with me?'

Olivia frowned. 'I—I thought I would go back to the Hayes' to change and freshen up a little.' She looked down ruefully at her creased clothing.

The girl nodded. 'Thank you for your help anyway, I mustn't impose on you any longer.'

Olivia was still worried about the young girl when she got back to the Hayes house, and yet Sally's last words had been a dismissal. What else could she do but be dismissed? What else did she want to do . . .?

Mrs Jenkins was a dear to nurse, not letting her illness

disrupt her life any more than it needed to be, having a vitality for life that couldn't be daunted by anything.

It was almost a month since Olivia had come to work for the elderly lady, a month when she hadn't been to see Marcus again, although Clara had told her that he was physically well again, that they were discharging him from hospital soon. Apparently Sally hadn't broken down as Olivia had suspected she would, instead she had become her father's eyes, spending most of her time with him.

Then one day out of the blue Sally called her to ask if they might meet. She didn't want to go; she had once again made her break away from the Hamilton family. But Sally was insistent, and as Olivia's patient was taking her afternoon rest she decided to see the young girl, arranging to meet at a coffee shop in town.

'It's about Daddy.' Sally came straight to the point once they had been served their coffee and left in privacy. She was a more mature Sally, her grey eyes intent, her body filled with a nervous energy.

Olivia instantly stiffened. 'What about him?'

Sally sighed, chewing on her inner lip. 'I—It's hard to explain.'

'Try,' Olivia encouraged softly.

'I'd rather you came and visited him, saw for yourself what's wrong with him.'

She swallowed hard, her lashes fluttering uncertainly over troubled green eyes. 'I don't think that would be a good idea.'

'But it would be better if you saw him,' Sally pleaded. 'I just can't explain what's wrong, except to say that he—he isn't himself.'

'He's blind, Sally. It will take time for him to adjust——'

'It isn't just that,' the girl shook her head. 'You would have to see him to know what I mean.'

'No——'

'Why can't you?' Sally cried. 'You said he didn't recognise you. You can just be a friend of mine, he doesn't have to know who you are.'

'I'm not dressed——'

'Daddy won't know what you're wearing,' Sally reminded her bitterly.

No, he wouldn't. Marcus wouldn't be able to see her casual denims and the loose silk top, her hair brushed about her shoulders in red-gold curls. He wouldn't be able to see any of that. 'All right,' she sighed her agreement. 'But I really don't know what you think I can do that the doctors can't.'

Her heart almost seemed to stop beating as she followed Sally into the private hospital room Marcus still occupied. The room was full of flowers, their perfume filling the room, but it was to the man sitting in the chair by the open window that her gaze was drawn. He sat perfectly still in the chair, faced towards the window, and yet seeing none of the smooth green lawn in front of him, the neat flower-beds, the bright sunshine making the buttercups on the lawn shine like pieces of gold, the sky above a deep clear blue, completely cloudless; a perfect summer's day, in fact.

And Marcus could see none of it, although the open window at least allowed him to hear the birds singing, to feel the warmth of the day. He sat stiffly in the chair, ramrod-straight, wearing black trousers and a light blue shirt, the latter short-sleeved. His body was leaner than a month ago, and although the cuts had healed on his face and the stitches had been removed, the bandage gone from about his head too, his face looked thinner too.

He turned as he heard them enter the room, and Olivia had to suppress her gasp as those familiar grey eyes looked straight at her—and then through her, reminding her that he really couldn't see her, that the specialist Simon Brooks had first called in had been uncertain if he would ever see again. The proposal that they have more tests done later, when the initial injury had healed, had been flatly refused by Marcus, deciding he would have no more examinations by any specialists.

His expression was harsh, his mouth a thin unhappy line, a bleak look to his eyes. 'Sally?' he queried sharply.

'Yes, Daddy,' she moved forward to kiss his cheek. 'I've brought you some fruit,' she told him lightly.

'Thank you.' His voice was emotionless as he once again turned back in the direction of the window.

'I'll put it in the bowl, shall I?' his daughter continued in a cheerful voice.

'Yes.'

Olivia hung back near the door, wishing she had never been persuaded to come here. It had been a mistake, there was nothing she could do to help Marcus.

Suddenly he stiffened, turning his face in her direction, a dark frown to his brow as he seemed to look directly at her. 'Is there someone else here?' he demanded harshly. 'Sally, is there someone with you?'

His daughter turned almost guiltily, although he couldn't possibly know of the emotion. 'I've brought a friend with me to see you.'

'A friend?' he probed savagely.

'Olivia.'

His nostrils flared out furiously, a white ring of anger about his compressed mouth. 'I'm not some damned peep-show!' he rasped.

'Daddy——'

'What do you think I am, Sally?' he said bitterly. 'Some sort of freak? What did you tell your little *friend* Olivia, "Come and see my father, he's blind"!'

Sally was white with shock, and she gave a strangulated cry before running from the room.

'Well?' he barked as he sensed Olivia was still in the

room. 'Aren't you going to run too?'

She wanted to, she wanted to run after Sally and comfort her. Marcus had hurt her terribly, and she didn't deserve his savage anger. 'I don't run, Mr Hamilton,' she told him calmly. 'Not from bullies like you, anyway,' she added challengingly.

Angry colour flooded his otherwise pale cheeks, the tan having faded from his cheeks after five weeks in hospital. 'Bully!' he repeated scornfully. 'How can I be a bully when I can't even *see* who I'm bullying?'

'You've just hurt the person who loves you most in the world.' Olivia walked further into the room. 'That makes you an emotional bully, Mr Hamilton. At least, in my book it does.'

'Maybe your opinion doesn't interest me,' he mocked harshly.

'Maybe you're going to get it anyway.' She was shaking so much she could hardly stand, but to run now wouldn't do this man any good.

He was Sally's father, so he could hurt the girl, he was the hospital's Chief Surgeon, and so he could command respect here—and from the look of him it wasn't doing him any good at all! He was withdrawn and unreasonable. And she knew that here lay Sally's problem, that Marcus wasn't 'himself'. He was making no effort to accept or combat his blindness. Bitterness was still his main emotion, and after five weeks he should be making some effort, *any* effort.

'Get out of here,' he told her with cold contempt.

'I haven't finished——'

'Oh, I think you have!'

'No,' she said firmly, 'I haven't. Sally's been concerned about you, and I can see why now. When are you going to stop feeling sorry for yourself and start to live again?'

'For what?' he bit out curtly.

'For Sally, for your mother-in-law, just for the hell

of it! You're a gifted man——'

'Oh, they've started employing blind surgeons now, have they?' he rasped, a muscle jerking erratically in his throat. 'I think not,' he derided.

'You may not always be blind.'

'And in the meantime you think I should keep my hand in? Would you like to volunteer to be my first patient?' he sneered. 'Would you?' he repeated harshly. 'I know which part of you I would like to cut out,' he taunted hardly.

'I can guess,' she said dryly. 'But surely you can see——'

'No, I *don't* see, that's the trouble.' He stood up in his agitation, stumbling over the chair as he turned.

Olivia moved instinctively to steady him, her hands on his arm as she felt him tense, instantly regretting her action as he went white with rage.

'Get your hands off me!' he grated through clenched teeth, pushing her away. 'Don't touch me!'

'Would you rather I'd let you fall?' she shouted back at him, two bright spots of angry colour in her cheeks as she glared at him, able to see the many scars that had been left on his face by the deep cuts now that she was so close to him. Some of them would always remain and some of them would fade altogether—but none of them mattered as much as his blindness.

'Maybe I would!'

'I'll remember that next time!'

'There won't be a next time for you! Get out of here!' He was shouting loudly now, groping his way over to the bed. 'Get out!' he repeated vehemently as he slumped down weakly on to the bed.

'Marcus——'

'What on earth is going on here?' A concerned Simon Brooks came into the room, Sally standing slightly behind him. 'I could hear shouting,' he frowned.

'Get that girl out of here,' Marcus told him through gritted teeth, his face averted.

'But——'

'Don't worry,' Olivia choked, 'I'm going. But if I were Sally,' she spoke to that averted face. 'I would tell you to go to hell!' With that she ran out of the room, leaning weakly against the wall outside, dry sobs racking her body.

'What on earth happened after I left?' Sally's concerned voice broke into Olivia's distressed state.

She straightened, calming herself with effort. 'Just your father losing his temper. Not for the first time, I'm sure,' she attempted to smile, although she was still shaken by the encounter.

'But it is,' Sally said eagerly. 'Usually he just sits there, hardly saying a word to anyone.'

'He certainly said a few to me,' Olivia said ruefully.

'I heard most of them,' Sally nodded. 'I could hardly believe it when he flew into a temper like that, it isn't like him at all.'

'It isn't like me either,' Olivia grimaced. 'I don't ever remember losing my temper like that before.'

'But it worked, don't you see?' Sally said excitedly. 'Your arguing with him brought him out of his apathy.'

'Perhaps,' she nodded. 'I have to go now, Sally. I have a patient to take care of—my own patient.'

'But——'

'I'm sorry, Sally, but I have to go,' she insisted jerkily. 'I—I hope your father feels better soon.'

She was in such a hurry to get away that she almost ran. Seeing Marcus again had been a mistake, one of many she seemed to have made lately.

And if she thought she had escaped the Hamilton family now she was mistaken. Sally called her every day for the next week, pleading with her for the two of them to meet again. Olivia always refused. And yet the memory of Marcus groping blindly in the darkness stayed with her. He was the proudest, most self-assured man she had ever known, and his anger at his blindness was all the stronger because of that. It was a pity he couldn't direct that anger at something other than himself.

Then to her surprise and dismay, Sally arrived to see her at Mrs Jenkins' house one afternoon—an act of desperation, she assured Olivia. 'I need your help,' she said quietly.

Olivia drew in a deep breath. The two of them were alone, Mrs Jenkins once again taking her rest. 'The last time I agreed to help you your father chewed me to pieces,' she reminded her.

'Exactly,' the girl nodded her satisfaction.

Olivia's eyes narrowed frowningly. 'Exactly ...?' she repeated warily, feeling as if she were being drawn into something that she may not get out of.

Sally sighed. 'After Daddy lost his temper so badly with you that afternoon I had high hopes of him coming out of his lethargy, of him starting to fight back. But that's remained the only time he's shown any reaction to anything. He just sits in a chair all day, all night too sometimes, answering us in that dull emotionless voice, as if he has no interest in anything. I thought he might be different when he came home——'

'He's home now?' Olivia couldn't help her interest.

'Yes,' the girl nodded. 'For the last four days. And he's stayed just the same. I just can't get through to him!'

'You will, in time.'

Sally shook her head. 'The doctor doesn't seem to think so. He says—he says Daddy is going into himself more and more each day. He thinks my father might have a complete nervous breakdown if something isn't done soon.'

Olivia swallowed hard. 'Psychiatric help——'

'Daddy won't let any more doctors in the house.'

She could see how her father's behaviour was affecting Sally; her pallor was even more noticeable, her look of defeat almost as pronounced as Marcus's himself. 'And Simon Brooks can't do anything?' she shook her head.

'He's tried.' Sally's hand trembled as she pushed her long hair back from her face. 'He's been a very good friend to us both, but he can't force Daddy to respond. But something you said the other day at the hospital gave me an idea.'

'Something *I* said?' Olivia's eyes were wide, deeply green, the lashes long and thick.

'You're a nurse, you have private patients——'

'Oh no, Sally,' she refused urgently even before the other girl could put her request into words. 'I already have a job. Besides, your father doesn't need a full-time nurse,' she added desperately.

'He does,' Sally nodded. 'We have one now.'

'Well, then . . .'

'And Daddy treats her as coldly as he does everyone and everything else,' the girl sighed.

Olivia frowned her puzzlement. 'I didn't realise he would have a nurse, I thought you said he was physically well?'

'He still tires very easily, and he's still under medication, sleeping pills mainly.' Sally drew in a deeply ragged breath. 'Mr Brooks doesn't think that he should have access to them.'

The colour drained from Olivia's face, leaving her very pale. 'He surely doesn't think——? I'll never believe that of your father!' she denied firmly.

'I wouldn't have done once either,' Sally said shakily. 'I wouldn't have believed it now if he hadn't told me himself that he wished he were dead.'

'It's a normal reaction——'

'Nothing about my father is *normal* at the moment,' the other girl told her heatedly. 'He's always despised weakness in others, especially when it comes to the taking of a life, and for him to even talk of wanting to die tells me he means it.'

'And what do you want me to do?' Olivia sighed.

'He's different with you, he fights back. And if he fights back then he won't break.'

'He fought back once, Sally,' Olivia reasoned. 'That doesn't mean he'll do it again.'

'Come and see him,' Sally suggested eagerly. 'Then we'll know for sure.'

'And if he doesn't respond that will be the end of it?'

'Yes,' Sally nodded, 'I promise. But if he does respond . . .?'

'I'm accompanying Mrs Jenkins on a cruise next week——'

'Oh, I see.' Sally had stiffened, standing up. 'I didn't realise a cruise would mean more to you than Daddy does!'

'It doesn't! Sally——'

'It sounded like it to me.' Sally's eyes glittered angrily. 'My father needs you——'

'You don't know that,' Olivia shook her head.

'And you obviously aren't willing to find out.' Sally gave her a disgusted look. 'If I offered to pay for a cruise for you after you've taken care of Daddy would you change your mind?'

Her breath caught in her throat at the desperate anger in the other girl's face, at the insult she had just given her. 'I'll come and see your father,' she told Sally coolly. 'See how he reacts to me. And then I'll talk to his doctor before I make any other decisions.'

Sally's face lit up. 'I can't thank you enough!'

'I haven't promised anything,' she warned. 'And, Sally . . .'

'Yes?' Sally looked at her eagerly.

'If you ever talk to me again the way you did a few minutes ago I'll slap you,' Olivia told the other girl quietly. 'Understood?'

Sally blushed, looking very young and unsure of herself. 'I'm sorry. But I'd do it again,' she added with a certain amount of defiance, 'if I thought it would help Daddy.'

Olivia gave a rueful smile at the other girl's honesty. 'I'm sure you would. But the only reason I mentioned the cruise was that it means that I could be free as from next week if I have to be. I'm sure Mrs Jenkins could get someone else to accompany her on the cruise. But if your father's reaction to me is as verbally violent as before I can't really see any doctor recommending that as being good for him,' she teased lightly.

'Mr Brooks seemed very interested in the idea when I suggested it to him.'

Olivia sighed, not at all surprised by the young girl's arrogant assumption that she would agree to help; there was more than a little of her father in Sally. 'When do you want me to come over? I have tomorrow off, if that's any help to you.'

'Perfect!' Sally said excitedly. 'Simon—Mr Brooks,' she amended with a blush, 'is coming over to examine Daddy in the morning. You could both stay to lunch afterwards and discuss my idea.'

'If I'm still in one piece!'

Sally giggled, instantly appearing younger. 'Don't worry, we'll pull you out before it goes that far.'

'Thanks!'

Sally moved to kiss her warmly. 'Thank you,' she said huskily. 'I'll see you tomorrow, about eleven-thirty?'

'I'll be there,' Olivia nodded, already regretting her decision.

She had been mad to agree to this. Marcus could hurt her so easily, seemed to take delight in being cruel to her, and it was a hurt she felt much more than he could ever realise. He had forgotten her very existence the last six years, even her name not evoking any memories, but how much more cruel his barbs could be if he should realise she was the young student nurse who had loved him so deeply all those years ago. But she had no reason to suppose he would ever remember that. And perhaps that was as well if she were to become his nurse!

She dressed with care the next day, wanting to look her best even if Marcus couldn't see her to appreciate that. The lemon sun-dress gave her the look of an exotic flower, her make-up was light, the perfume she wore smelled of spring flowers.

Her tension rose as she was shown into the lounge by the housekeeper. Sybil Carr rose gracefully to her feet, more composed today, her make-up and appearance once again perfect. 'Sally is upstairs with Marcus's doctor,' she informed her coolly.

This was the Sybil Carr she was used to, the light jersey dress flattering the slimness of her figure, her hair professionally styled.

'Would you care for tea?' Sybil offered distantly.

'I——'

At that moment Sally came into the room accompanied by the young doctor, both of them looking very serious, although Sally's expression brightened as she saw Olivia had arrived. 'I'm so glad to see you,' she smiled tremulously.

'Your father . . .?'

'There's no change,' Sally sighed.

'And no change in this case . . .' Simon trailed off pointedly. 'Nice to meet you again, Miss King,' he smiled. 'Although I wish it could be in happier circumstances.'

'Sally has explained to you why she wants me to see her father?' She was watching him closely, her training as a nurse showing her just how worried he was.

'Yes,' he nodded. 'And I can't see that it's going to do any harm. You'll know when he's had enough?'

'Of course.'

'I'll take you up,' Sally offered instantly. 'I'm sure Grandmother will give you some tea, Mr Brooks. I won't be long.'

Olivia walked up the stairs with the younger girl, too nervous about seeing Marcus again to engage in a conversation. She hadn't slept all night through nervousness about this meeting, and she was as jumpy as a nervous kitten as she stood outside his bedroom door.

'Why isn't he downstairs with the family?' she frowned. 'Surely he doesn't stay up here on his own all the time?'

Sally nodded. 'He refuses to leave his bedroom.'

'Why?'

'He doesn't say why, he just refuses to come down.' She shrugged. 'You know Daddy.'

She *had* known him, but this didn't sound like him at all. 'Does he eat in his room too?'

'I told you, he never goes downstairs.'

Olivia drew in a determined breath, fighting down her nervousness, ready to face Marcus now. 'Does he know I'm going to see him?'

'Are you kidding!' Sally gave a scornful laugh. 'I might have got something thrown at me!'

'Nice to know I induce such a pleasant mood in someone,' she grimaced.

'Olivia, I've spoken to the nurse about the possibility of your coming to work here——'

'You shouldn't have done that,' she said impatiently. 'Nothing has been decided yet.' She made the claim, and yet she was very certain that the decision was being taken out of her hands, that in the end she would have no say in the matter.

'I just wanted to smooth the way if you did decide to come,' Sally explained in a pleading voice. 'She's agreed to leave as soon as you take over.'

Olivia shook her head in exasperation. 'We'll see,' she sighed. 'And if you hear me scream——'

'We'll come running,' Sally grinned. 'Good luck!'

'I have a feeling I'm going to need it!'

She heard Sally giggle behind her as she opened the door and softly entered the room. It was a large room, mainly in brown and white, the carpet a deep rich brown, as was the quilt cover on the double bed, the paper on one wall in a small brown and white pattern, several paintings on the other white painted walls, mainly seascapes.

But these were all trivialities to Olivia, it was the man sitting in front of the window that once again held her attention, his face turned sightlessly up at the sky, dark glasses shielding his eyes this time, the rest of his face harshly composed. She didn't like the dark glasses, she felt as if part of him was hidden from her by them.

He turned as he heard the door close with a firm click. 'Anna?' he barked.

She assumed Anna must be the nurse. 'No,' she denied huskily.

His face tightened. 'Who is it?' he rasped.

Olivia walked slowly across the room, her dress moving smoothly against her body before she stopped next to the window. 'It's a lovely day,' she told him softly. 'You must have a wonderful gardener, he's managed to get a beautiful display of flowers and still leave them looking wild, not set in those neat little rows. Oh, and there's a dog in the garden,' she had just seen the Golden Labrador chasing a butterfly. 'Is he yours?' she asked interestedly, unwillingly noticing how attractive he looked in brown trousers and tan-coloured shirt.

'What are you doing here?' His tone was savage. 'Have you come to tell me again to stop feeling sorry for myself?' His mouth twisted with derision. 'To start living again?'

He remembered her from last time! 'Did you recognise my voice?'

'Did you think I wouldn't?' he mocked harshly. 'That hard little voice that told me to live again when there is nothing to live for.'

Olivia bit her tongue to stop her angry retort. 'There isn't when all you do is sit in that chair and brood all day, no.'

'What else should I do?' Marcus rasped bitterly. 'Read a book? Watch television?'

'There are plenty of things a blin—you can do,' she bit her bottom lip as she saw the way he had flinched.

'A blind person,' he finished for her savagely. 'Name one?' he challenged harshly.

'You could go out for walks, sit out in the garden, go out for drives, eat with the rest of the family. That's plenty of things to be going on with,' she said briskly. 'Until you get your strength back.'

'I don't think so,' he refused hardly. 'There's no reason to walk in the garden when you can't see it, the same goes for sitting in it. As for driving, I hate being driven by someone else. And as far as eating with the rest of the family goes,' he derided, 'what happens when I spill my food down my shirt-front, or knock wine over someone? Do we just laugh it off, Miss King?' His voice was harsh. 'I think not. As for the dog—yes, he's mine. Unfortunately he doesn't happen to be a "seeing" dog. Do you have any more bright ideas?' he taunted.

'Plenty,' she nodded. 'You certainly can't stay in this room for the rest of your life.'

'Why can't I?'

'Because—Because you just can't. Your blindness may not be permanent——'

'I've never lived on false promises before, and I'm not about to start now!'

'But you've too active a mind to want to sit here for the rest of your life!'

'Have I?' he scorned.

'Yes,' she bit out, his apathy angering her.

'And how would you know that, Miss King?' he taunted. 'You don't even know me, you met me only a week ago. You're a friend of my daughter, nothing more, and I don't have to take this well-meaning advice from you.' He turned away dismissively, the sunlight highlighting the sharp angles of his face.

He really didn't remember her from six years ago, his words of just now more than proved that. 'You're wrong, Mr Hamilton,' she told him with renewed confidence. 'I'm more than just Sally's friend, I'm also a nurse. Your nurse,' she added softly.

'Like hell you are!' He turned on her savagely, his fingers tightly gripping the arms of the chair, his knuckles white.

'Oh, but I am,' she said with breezy assurance. 'As from Monday morning you will have this "hard little voice" telling you night and day to start living again.'

Marcus stood up, moving surely across the room, evidence that he had Brailled it meticulously the last five days. He wrenched open the door and stood back pointedly. Olivia made no effort to go through the open doorway, and it became a battle of wills to see who would give in first. She had no intention of being the one to give in, if she did she would never win against him again.

'I want you to go,' he told her through gritted teeth.

'I know,' she replied evenly.

'Well?' he barked.

'We haven't finished discussing my employment as your nurse, Mr Hamilton,' she told him with a calmness she was far from feeling.

'You are mistaken, Miss King,' he bit out forcefully. 'There is no employment to discuss.'

'I've been employed by your daughter——'

'My daughter doesn't run this house, Miss King, I do.'

'Really?' Olivia queried softly, knowing that now was a time to remain insensitive to his disability, even to taunt him with it. 'I would say you're doing very little of anything hiding yourself up here.'

Marcus closed the door with savage force. 'What did you say?' he ground out.

She made her voice sound light and conversational, knowing she couldn't allow him to know of the tears swimming in her eyes. 'Sally is very young to have this sudden responsibility, but I think she's coping very well. Of course, she shouldn't have to cope with it at all, but she has no choice, does she? So, until you can physically throw me out of the house, I will continue to work for your daughter.'

Marcus was very white, breathing raggedly. 'Get out of here,' he ordered weakly. 'Just leave.'

This time she did go to the door, knowing that he had indeed 'had enough'. 'I'll be with you on Monday morning, Mr Hamilton,' she told him lightly.

He didn't answer her, but bent over defeatedly, Olivia finally allowing the tears to fall as she leant back against the wall outside.

Hurting Marcus was the hardest thing she had ever had to do—besides leaving him that first time, although then she had had no choice, knowing she had no place in his life now his wife was back. Today she had chosen to hurt him, and it had hurt her more.

Sally sat on the top step of the stairs, standing up as Olivia continued to cry, her arms going wordlessly about her shoulders as she comforted her.

'You heard?' Olivia choked.

'Yes,' the younger girl confirmed huskily.

'I had to do it. I didn't want to, but I had to.'

'Yes,' Sally said again, 'I know that.'

'I wish your father did. Oh, Sally, I can't do this,' Olivia shook her head. 'I'm hurting myself as much as Marcus. I would have given anything to put my arms around him and cry.'

'I've already done that,' the other girl said quietly. 'It doesn't do any good. He just patted my hand and told me not to worry. Not to worry!' she scorned shakily. 'I've done nothing else since the accident. And Grandmother does nothing to help, she can't even bring herself to visit him. He needs someone like you, Olivia, to make him fight. I need someone like you too,' she added quietly. 'Please, Olivia, you're my last hope.'

Olivia couldn't ignore the pleading in those grey eyes, eyes so like Marcus's she felt like crying again. 'I'm not sure . . .' She knew her hesitation was a sign she was beginning to give in.

'You told Daddy you'd be here on Monday morning,' Sally eagerly picked up that weakening. 'If you don't turn up he's going to think he's won, that he frightened you away.'

'Yes,' Olivia sighed heavily, knowing the other girl was right, knowing herself that she had given in at that moment. 'Although Mr Brooks has the final say on whether or not I should be Marcus's nurse,' she warned.

'He'll say you should,' Sally said with conviction.

Olivia had a feeling he would too!

CHAPTER FOUR

MONDAY morning dawned bright and sunny, and Olivia determinedly kept her thoughts on the beauty of the day as she ate her breakfast alone with Sally, Sybil Carr having hers on a tray in her room. In fact the older woman had more or less made herself absent from the time Olivia had arrived at the house the evening before.

Olivia had insisted Sally should go to college today. 'Life has to return to normal,' she told the younger girl as she voiced her misgivings over breakfast. 'Besides, if your father believes himself to be alone in the house with me he might be less inclined to want to throw me out.'

'I wouldn't count on it,' Sally grimaced. 'He hasn't mentioned knowing you're in the house, but he's been in a terrible temper since last night.'

Olivia gave a rueful smile. 'Then he does know I'm here.'

'I think so,' the younger girl nodded, glancing at her wrist-watch. 'I'd better be going. Are you sure you'll be all right?'

'Very sure,' she smiled. 'I've had worse patients than your father.' Although she couldn't for the life of her remember when! Some of her patients had been difficult, even goodnatured Rick Hayes at first, but none of them had been quite as formidable as Marcus proved to be.

Simon Brooks had been all for her taking over the care of his patient, sure that in time the anger he displayed only to her would bring about some sort of result. Olivia only hoped it would be a favourable one!

74

She hesitated outside the door to Marcus's bedroom, wondering what sort of reception she was going to get. If what Sally had said about his temper was true he wasn't going to put out the Welcome mat!

He was already out of bed and dressed, sitting by the window as she entered after a brief knock. He didn't even turn as she entered the room, as if he knew who it was before she came in.

'Why do you wear those glasses when there's nothing wrong with the look of your eyes?' Olivia attacked as she walked across the room to his side.

Instead of the anger she had been hoping to evoke his mouth twisted into a mocking smile. 'And why do you wear that uniform when you know I can't see how efficient you look in it?'

Hot colour flooded her cheeks. 'I—Well, I—How did you——?'

'Know?' he finished tauntingly. 'It moves crisply as you walk. Starchy, like you,' he added insultingly.

That was better! 'You didn't answer my question about the glasses,' Olivia reminded him abruptly.

'I wear them because I want to wear them.'

'That's no answer at all!'

'It's the only one you're going to get,' he drawled. 'You didn't answer me about the uniform.'

'I'm a nurse——'

'So you've already told me,' he derided. '*My* nurse. And I would prefer it if you didn't wear a uniform when you're with me. Take it off.'

Colour flooded her cheeks, her eyes wide. 'I beg your pardon?'

'My dear Miss King,' he drawled mockingly, 'what do you think I meant? You're staying at the house, aren't you?'

'Yes.'

'Then it should be a simple matter for you to go to your room and change into something else.' His expression suddenly became bleak. 'Although you could take the damned thing off here for all the good it would do me! Even the pleasure of looking at a beautiful woman has been denied me.'

'I'm not beautiful,' she dismissed.

'But I'll never know that, will I?' he rasped. 'You could weigh twenty stone and look like Godzilla for all I know!'

'I'm not quite that ugly,' she smiled. 'You don't have to see a woman's beauty,' she gently tried to ease his bitterness. 'You can always feel it.'

'Oh yes,' he derided harshly, 'I'm sure any woman would just love me to grope my way over her body. Would you like it, Miss King?' he scorned.

Olivia bit her bottom lip, not sure she would be able to withstand the intimacy that would call for.

'I thought not,' Marcus taunted hardly.

She drew in a deep controlling breath, knowing that this was her first real test, that she had to treat this case as professionally as if she didn't know Marcus, hadn't once loved him. 'I'll make a deal with you,' she told him briskly.

He stiffened, his expression suddenly wary. 'What sort of deal?'

'You take off the dark glasses, they aren't necessary for you anyway, and you have perfectly nice eyes—and I'll let you Braille me. Is it a deal?' she asked audaciously.

Marcus seemed to think about it for some time, then he nodded slowly. 'Deal,' he said abruptly. 'Although I could be letting myself in for a disappointment.' He sat forward in his chair, looking up at her expectantly.

Olivia moved to kneel in front of him. 'Disappointment?' she questioned.

'You have a very sexy voice, Miss King.' He gave a twisted smile. 'How sad if I find it belongs to the Godzilla creature after all!'

She smiled, then took his hands, the long sensitive hands that still bore the marks of his scars, and put them either side of her face, knowing that it was only natural he should want to know what the person behind the voice looked like. If only she didn't feel quite so nervous about it—the thought of Marcus touching her so intimately made her breathing soft and shallow.

He touched her hair first. 'Hm, nice. Soft and curly. Colour?'

'Sort of reddish-gold,' she supplied breathlessly. His fingertips were featherlight on her face now, her skin sensitive to his every touch.

He was so absorbed in his task, she hoped he didn't sense her trembling. 'Nice eyebrows,' he murmured. 'And long silky lashes. What colour eyes?'

'Green?'

'Deep green, or the green of——'

'Deep green,' she supplied abruptly, his breath warm against her face.

'An upturned nose,' he mused as his finger ran the length of it. 'Freckles?'

'A few,' she confirmed, her discomfort increased by the amount of time he took over each feature.

'High cheekbones,' he continued. 'Hollow cheeks, so you aren't twenty stone,' he mocked.

'Eight,' she supplied curtly. 'And I'm five feet eight inches tall.'

'That's too thin for your height,' he frowned. 'No wonder your cheeks are hollow! It's a nice mouth,' he touched the lower lip, parting them slightly. 'Mmm, very kissable.'

It took all her will power not to pull away from the intimacies he was subjecting her to, but she knew by the derisive twist of his mouth that he was deliberately goading her. She remained silent with effort.

'Has it been kissed often, Olivia?' he rasped suddenly.

'Occasionally,' she amended stiffly.

His fingers moved abruptly to her chin. 'Determined,' he decided. 'But then I knew it would be,' he murmured, touching her ears now. 'Pretty,' he nodded, and his hands dropped away. 'You're a very beautiful woman, Olivia. Stand up now,' he instructed.

'You're finished?' she asked with some relief.

He shook his head. 'You have to be standing when I Braille your body.'

She gasped. 'No!'

His expression hardened. 'That was the deal, Olivia,' he said harshly.

'No——'

'Yes,' he insisted tautly. 'I asked if you would mind my groping my way over your body, and you said I could Braille you if I discarded the glasses you've taken such an aversion to.'

The hot colour in her cheeks wouldn't be dispelled. 'I meant my face, not my body!' she gasped.

Marcus's mouth thinned. 'So you're backing out of the deal?'

'It wasn't the one I made, and you know it wasn't!'

'Pity.' He sat back in his chair, as if the subject weren't important to him. 'You're too thin for my tastes, anyway,' he added insultingly.

It was even more of an insult than he knew. Olivia remembered clearly the voluptuous wife he had preferred to her six years ago.

'Well?' he barked as she still knelt in front of him.

She stood up, looking down to see the bitterness etched into his harsh face. And those damned glasses—how she hated them! But enough to withstand Marcus's hands on her body? Cruel as it might seem, at least he wouldn't be able to see her blushes! 'All right,' she snapped, 'you can Braille my body too.'

A pulse jerked erratically in his jaw, but he made no effort to move. 'I'm not that desperate,' he dismissed coldly, and stood up, and as Olivia hadn't yet moved, walked straight into her. 'I'm sorry.' His hands came out to steady her with ill-concealed impatience, moving sharply away. 'Here, take the damned glasses if it's that important to you.' He held them out to her.

Olivia took them, seeing that the strain in his eyes had increased the last few days. 'I'll just go and change out of my uniform. I thought we could go for a walk in the garden——'

'No.'

She frowned. 'No?'

'I told you before,' he bit out curtly. 'There's no point to it.'

'I think there is.' She was just as stubborn. 'Besides, you can renew your acquaintance with Jasper. I met him last night, he's lovely.' She had found the dog to be very friendly, although Sally said he was pining for Marcus. 'He isn't eating properly, you know,' she told him. 'He misses you.'

'Dogs are fickle creatures—like women,' he added hardly. 'He'll soon transfer his love to someone else.'

There was a wealth of bitterness in his words, showing that he might have loved his wife enough to take her back, but that he had never forgotten her defection.

'But he doesn't need to, does he?' she persisted. 'Not when he still has you.'

Marcus looked really angry now, his mouth tight, his eyes narrowed. 'I don't want the dog up here, and I don't want to go down to the garden! For God's sake *just—leave—me—alone!*'

'I can't do that.' Olivia gave him a close look. 'Did you shave this morning?'

He frowned. 'What does that have to do with Jasper?'

'Nothing. I just wondered——'

'Well, don't,' he snapped. 'I don't need a nursemaid. I'm completely bathroom trained,' he taunted. 'I went through all that at the hospital. I was also taught how to dress myself. So why the sudden interest in whether or not I've shaved?' He touched the lean smoothness of his chin, not a nick or missed whisker anywhere.

'It's very good,' Olivia assured him. 'I was just wondering why, when you can do complicated things like washing, shaving and dressing yourself, you wouldn't go for a simple walk in the garden.'

'Because I refuse to stumble about with a white stick, that's why!' he told her savagely.

Why hadn't she thought of that? Marcus was much too proud to let anyone see him in such a vulnerable position. He had Brailled this bedroom and the adjoining bathroom, knew every inch of them, but the garden was an unknown quantity to him, full of unseen hazards he didn't even want to try and challenge. She was so new at dealing with the psychology of a newly blinded person; she had only dealt with it briefly during her general training as a nurse. She had told all this to Simon Brooks, but he hadn't seemed to think it was important. The previous nurse had been highly trained in this field, and yet getting no response from Marcus at all. Olivia just wished she didn't feel quite so much as if she were moving in the dark too!

'I have something much better than a white stick,' she told him cheerfully.

'Oh yes?' he sneered.

'Yes.' She remained unperturbed by his scorn. 'Try this.' She put her hand into his, feeling him flinch away from her. 'Or this if you prefer,' she put her hand through the crook of his arm. 'It should be quite simple for me to give you the instructions you need.'

'No!'

'Why not?' she sighed.

'Because I'm perfectly happy where I am,' he rasped.

Her mouth set in an angry line. 'Maybe you are— but I'm not! I have no intention of spending all the summer in this stuffy room when there's all that lovely garden I could be sitting in.'

'Running away, Miss King?' he taunted.

'Not at all,' she replied calmly. 'I just think Jasper would appreciate my company more than you do.'

'Undoubtedly,' he drawled.

Olivia shot him a glare of frustration before leaving the room, her heart beating faster in her agitation. After saying she was going to the garden it would have given him a victory to think he had swayed her to his will if she stayed. He might think he had her running, but she hadn't finished yet by a long way!

She changed into denims and a dark green tee-shirt before going doownstairs, to find Jasper already out in the garden, coming over to greet her exuberantly.

'Your moody master is still sulking in his room,' she said in a loud voice, conscious of the still figure sitting behind the open window upstairs. 'So it's just you and me, boy. Let's find you a stick to play with, hmm?'

For the next hour she and Jasper had great fun playing together, Olivia making sure Marcus knew exactly how much she and the dog were enjoying themselves. Although she didn't have to try very hard; Jasper was a delightful dog, very gentle, very friendly, and she felt as regretful as he looked when it was time for her to go back inside.

'I know, boy,' she stroked his golden coat. 'But I have to get back to work now. Perhaps tomorrow, okay?'

She went straight up to her room next to Marcus's to wash and tidy herself before lunch, her cheeks glowing with health, her eyes bright and clear as she went back down to the kitchen where the housekeeper was just serving lunch.

'I'll take Mr Hamilton's up with mine, if you like,' Olivia offered.

Miss Podmore looked uncertain. 'I usually give Mr Hamilton his on a tray.'

She nodded. 'We'll both have it on a tray.'

'I don't think Mr Hamilton will like that.'

'I don't suppose he will,' Olivia agreed lightly.

The housekeeper gave her a puzzled look. 'You don't seem worried by that.'

'I'm not.'

'Well—all right,' the middle-aged woman shrugged, putting the covers over their food and putting both meals on the same tray. 'But don't say I didn't warn you,' she added ruefully.

'I won't,' Olivia laughed, carrying the tray upstairs, knocking on Marcus's bedroom door with her foot, the tray too big to balance in one hand.

'Come in,' he called.

'I can't!' she shouted back.

'What the hell——' She could hear mutterings, and then the door was opened.

She sailed past him with the tray. 'Lunch,' she told him lightly, although all this cheerfulness was starting to be a strain. She was going to be worn out by it all by the end of the day!

Marcus moved to join her at the small table by the window. 'I thought you were a nurse, not a waitress,' he sneered.

Olivia arranged the food on the table, automatically telling him where she put everything. 'I'm not going to argue with you now,' she told him softly. 'I won't allow you to ruin my appetite. The pork looks delicious.'

'Then at least you won't starve, will you?' he derided.

'No.' She made herself comfortable in the chair opposite his. 'Aren't you going to sit down?' She looked up at him.

He gave an arrogant inclination of his head. 'When you've gone.'

'Oh, but I'm not going.'

'I don't need an audience while I eat!' Marcus ground out, his face rigid.

'You aren't getting one.' She put salt and pepper on her own food. 'I shall be too busy eating to watch you.'

'Eating——?' He turned sharply towards her. 'You aren't eating in here!'

'I've already started. I was right, the pork is delicious. Why don't you try some? I'm sure you——'

'Stop treating me like a child!'

'Then stop acting like one!' She raised her own voice to meet his. 'It isn't going to hurt you to eat lunch with me. I hate to eat alone.'

'Sybil——'

'Is lunching with friends.'

'She would be,' he muttered, evidence that he wasn't ignorant of the fact that his mother-in-law couldn't bring herself to even visit him, despite living in the same house.

'Please sit down, Marcus,' Olivia pleaded softly. 'The food is getting cold.'

He looked down at her fiercely for several long minutes—and it was difficult to believe those piercing grey eyes couldn't actually see her! Finally he sat down. 'Aren't you going to cut my food up for me?' he taunted.

'Do you want me to?' she challenged.

His mouth tightened. 'No.'

In fact he managed very well, better than a lot of people who could actually see what they were eating! Not that she made any comment about it, knowing he would resent that as being patronising.

'I'll get our coffee,' she told him after clearing away the tray.

Marcus had his back towards her, his body tense. 'Olivia . . .'

'Yes?' She turned at the door.

'Thank you,' the word seemed forced out of him. 'It was nice to know what I was eating for a change, and exactly where it was on the plate. Miss Podmore usually just leaves the tray and forgets to mention those vital facts. I once ate my horseradish sauce with my apple pie,' he revealed derisively.

'Oh, Marcus!'

'Get the coffee,' he ordered harshly.

By the time Olivia returned with the tray of coffee the moment of closeness had passed and Marcus was once more growling at her. But it had been a start, and she very wisely didn't push things any further, offering to read the newspaper to him later in the afternoon.

'I listen to the radio,' he dismissed the suggestion.

'But they don't give much more than the headlines,' she pointed out reasonably. 'Besides, I never have the time to read the newspaper myself.'

'So you want to read it in my time?'

'Why not?' she shrugged. 'I played with the dog in your time.'

His mouth twisted. 'While "his moody master sulked in his room".'

Olivia's mouth quirked. She had wondered if he had heard that remark. At the time she had meant him to, but now it seemed rather a childish thing for her to have said.

'Jasper would have preferred you to have gone down.'

'I'm sure he enjoyed your company just as much,' Marcus dismissed. 'You sounded as if you were having fun.'

'We were. Now shall I read the newspaper to you or not?' She was aware that he had deliberatly lead her away from her original question.

'Go ahead,' he invited mockingly. 'I'd hate to ruin a perfect day for you.'

Once again she decided to ignore his sarcasm, and read out the items she thought would interest him. At first he let her read without comment, then he would query her on certain points, until in the end she could tell he was listening to her intently.

'That's enough for now.' She put the newspaper down after an hour, seeing he was beginning to tire. 'I could do with a cup of tea, how about you?'

Marcus seemed to stiffen. 'I'm sorry, I didn't think. Please, go down and have your tea.'

'I'll bring it up here——'

'I would prefer to be on my own now.' Once again he was withdrawing from her. 'And I would prefer to have my dinner alone too.'

'Of course.' Olivia calmly accepted his dismissal of her, knowing she had won enough battles for today. 'But I'll bring it up, shall I? That way I can tell you what it is.'

'Very well,' he accepted abruptly, turning away from her.

Sally was just coming in from college as Olivia reached the bottom of the stairs, her expression one of anxiety. 'Everything all right?' she asked breathlessly, seeming to have run all the way home.

'Fine,' she answered noncommittally. She didn't want to raise Sally's hopes over what little progress she had made today, knowing that it could all be forgotten by tomorrow. Marcus was going to be far from an easy patient. 'Why don't you go up and see your father?' she suggested. 'I'm sure he would like that.'

Sally was halfway up the stairs before she came to

an abrupt halt, turning round to look at Olivia. 'Has he—has he been—all right?'

'Well, he hasn't thrown anything at me, if that's what you mean,' Olivia smiled.

Sally looked taken aback. 'I didn't think he would have done. Daddy isn't violent—except with his tongue,' she added ruefully. 'Then he can be pretty cutting.'

'I've noticed,' Olivia grimaced. 'How did college go today?'

'All right,' the girl shrugged. 'I was a bit preoccupied, though.'

'Because of your father,' she sympathised. 'Well, you can stop worrying now, your father and I are going to get along just fine,' she said with much more confidence than she actually felt. 'You just concentrate on your studies. Your father will be angry if you do badly because of his accident.' She knew Marcus well enough to be sure of that. 'What are you studying for, by the way?' she asked interestedly.

Sally gave an impish grin. 'Guess!'

'Not to enter the medical profession?' groaned Olivia.

With a light laugh Sally ran the rest of the way up the stairs. 'What else?'

'Indeed,' Olivia agreed dryly. 'I'll see you later.'

Sally paused at the door to her father's room. 'Is it safe to go in?' she asked conspiratorially.

'It would be less safe to stay outside!' her father barked from within.

'Whoops!' Sally was giggling as she entered the room.

Olivia smiled, going through to the kitchen to tell Miss Podmore Marcus and Sally would like their tea, ordering her own to be brought into the lounge. After the tense day she had had trying to keep one step ahead of Marcus, a cup of tea was the least reward she could give herself.

Sally had remained with her father, so everything appeared to be all right there. She sat back with her eyes closed, the weariness of the day washing over her. This job was going to be far from easy, and this was only the beginning!

'Making yourself comfortable, Miss King?' taunted a harsh female voice.

Her eyes were wary as she raised her lids. 'Mrs Carr,' she nodded acknowledgment of the other woman, sitting up straighter in the chair.

Sybil's mouth twisted. 'I must say, you don't exactly look the part.'

'The part?' Olivia frowned her puzzlement.

'You're supposed to be Marcus's nurse, Olivia.' Sybil came further into the room, the ravages of the last weeks completely erased from her perfectly made-up face and styled hair, her pale grey suit looking like real silk. She put her parcels down on the table before moving to sit in the chair opposite Olivia. 'He can hardly appreciate how attractive you look with that tee-shirt against the brightness of your hair, or the way your denims fit you like a second skin,' she scorned.

Olivia sensed the anger in the other woman, and she knew that here was a second member of the household who would prefer it if she weren't here. 'I dressed like this to please myself, Mrs Carr,' she replied coolly, 'not Marcus.'

'Did you?'

'Yes!'

Sybil's mouth twisted with mocking humour. 'Wouldn't a uniform be more appropriate?'

'Marcus would prefer me not to wear one,' she replied truthfully.

'And you still want to do what Marcus likes?'

Olivia stiffened at the other woman's insulting tone. 'Mr Hamilton is my patient, of course I want to do what's best for him,' she defended tautly.

'My dear, it's obvious that you and Marcus were once—close. Just don't trade on that, and his—blindness.' Sybil obviously had trouble just saying the word, confirming Olivia's suspicion that the older woman preferred not to accept Marcus's blindness, to ignore it and hope it would go away. 'Marcus has been far from celibate since Ruth's death,' she continued haughtily. 'He's a man who has need of a woman in his life, and as you're available . . .' she trailed off pointedly.

The pressure of Olivia's fingers into the arm of her chair increased as each insulting word left the other woman's red-painted mouth. 'Just what are you implying, Mrs Carr?' she asked tightly.

'Don't be naïve,' Sybil snapped. 'You and Marcus were lovers once, and now that he's blind——'

'You think I intend sleeping with him as part of my nursing duties?' Olivia stood up agitatedly.

'I'm sure it wouldn't be the first time,' Sybil drawled.

Olivia's face was deeply flushed, her eyes fever-bright. 'Then you know more than I do, Mrs Carr. I do not sleep with my patients, and neither am I "available". I never have been! Marcus and I have never been lovers either, but even if we had it's none of your business. As for sleeping with him now, you're wrong about that too. I'm here as Marcus's nurse, nothing more.'

'No?'

'No!'

Sybil shrugged, having lost none of her supreme self-confidence. 'I'm sure Marcus will be disappointed.'

'I would say the last thing on his mind at the

moment is going to bed with any woman! You know nothing of what he's feeling, you haven't even been to see him since the accident! I'm sorry,' Olivia gasped as the other woman seemed to blanch, 'I didn't mean to say that.'

'Didn't you?' Sybil snapped. 'I think you meant exactly what you said. Well, at least now we know where we stand, Olivia.'

She eyed the other woman warily. 'We do?'

'Oh yes.' Sybil's head went back in challenge. 'I didn't like you before, and I don't like you now.' She stood up, and the two women faced each other across the room like adversaries—which was precisely what they were, Olivia realised that now! 'As soon as Marcus is feeling more his old self again I will see that you leave here.'

'More his old self?' Olivia echoed slowly. 'You mean when he can see again?'

'Of course.'

'And if he never does?'

'You can't really know Marcus very well if you believe that,' Sybil scoffed. 'He has the will and determination to get through anything. He'll see again, you can be sure of that.'

Olivia watched the other woman leave, wondering if Sybil Carr could really be so sure of Marcus's determination. Right now his anger was directed at everyone, even himself, with no thought of regaining his sight.

But Sally seemed somewhat assured when she came downstairs a few minutes later, a smile lightening her features. 'He actually sat and talked to me!' she said excitedly. 'Took an interest, you know.'

Olivia did know, and it was a definite step forward. But she still gave no indication to Sally as to the progress of the day. Marcus was just as likely to be ordering her out of the house again tomorrow! And many more conversations like the one she had just had with Sybil Carr and she was likely to take him up on the suggestion!

She changed for dinner that evening, aware that Sally and Sybil would be doing so. Her dress was a practical 'little black dress', suitable for any evening occasion, and with her lack of evening clothes it was likely to get a lot of use here! It was halter-necked in style, leaving her shoulders and back bare, clinging to her firm breasts and narrow thighs. It gave her an unconscious elegance, and she returned Miss Podmore's smile warmly as she went into the kitchen to get Marcus's tray.

He still sat by the window as she let herself into the room, in spite of the sky darkening to dusk. It reminded Olivia all too poignantly that Marcus couldn't see that night was falling, that it was all darkness to him.

He had turned at the sound of the door opening, standing up to pull the brown velvet curtains. His mouth twisted as he turned back to her, as if he sensed her surprise. 'You've brought my dinner, so it must be getting dark outside. Isn't that right—Olivia?'

Without his dark glasses as a shield it seemed incredible that those piercing grey eyes couldn't see her. 'How did you know it was me?' Her tone was brisk as she arranged his dinner out on the table.

He shrugged, moving confidently towards her. 'Your perfume.'

She frowned. 'But it's new, I've never worn it before.'

'I said *your* perfume, Olivia.' He was standing very close now, his breath stirring the hair at her temple. 'I meant your body perfume. You smell of the earth, the moon and the sky. A sensual Aphrodite, in fact.'

'Oh.'

'Nothing else to say?' he taunted.

She was blushing too much to think of anything else *to* say. It was true people had body odours all of their own, she was aware of the deep musky smell of Marcus that spoke of his masculinity. But just thinking about that reminded her all too forcefully of Sybil Carr's accusations of this afternoon. She had never shared Marcus's bed, the other woman had been wrong about that, but she had wanted to. *God*, how she had wanted to! And looking at him now she realised that hadn't changed. He still excited her, still made her pulse race.

Instead of answering him she began to describe his dinner to him, studiously avoiding looking at him. These feelings of attraction she had for him wouldn't do; Marcus was her patient, and that was all he was, all he could ever be to her now.

'Coward,' he murmured at her lack of reply to his question.

'Not at all,' she answered strongly. 'I just don't happen to think this type of conversation serves any real purpose.'

'You're quite right, Olivia,' he derided. 'Conversation never serves a purpose. I've always believed actions speak louder than words.' Before she could even guess at his intention he had swept her up against him, his mouth finding hers with unerring accuracy.

She wanted to struggle, she tried to do so, but her body betrayed her, curving into the hardness of his as if it knew no other master. With a hungry groan her lips parted beneath his.

'What are you wearing?' Marcus groaned against her throat. 'Describe it to me.' His lips were like fire as they travelled the length of her throat to her shoulders, biting erotically against the soft skin there.

'I—It's a black dress——' She was having trouble articulating, her body on fire for the intimacy of his touch after being denied him for so long.

'Halter-necked.' His sure fingers moved to the single button fastening at her nape, easily releasing it, and the material fell down about her waist. 'I like the feel of your skin better. Although I'm sure the bright beauty of your hair looks very effective against the dress.'

'How did you——'

'You told me, remember?' His mouth moved back to hers, the pressure almost savage this time, as one hand moved up to capture the firm tautness of her breast.

Olivia knew and regretted the reason for his savagery, knew that for the few brief minutes he had made love to her his blindness had been forgotten, unimportant. He was making love to her with his hands, not his eyes. But she had unwittingly reminded him by her thoughtless question, and now she was being made to pay for that with his fierceness.

Marcus was brutal with her, not intent on arousing her but on punishing her. His mouth plundered hers roughly, with an intimacy that left her gasping. And all the time his hands were caressing the aching tips of her breasts, the dusky red auriole hardening beneath his pleasure-giving fingertips.

And that was the trouble, she *did* feel pleasure, even in the pain. She shouldn't, but she did. It had been so long since she had been with him like this, so long . . .

Marcus's mouth eased on hers as he sensed her surrender, his caresses more subtle now, his hands moving from her breast to her thigh in searching appreciation, his lips tasting hers, asking for her response—a response she was only too eager to give. This hadn't changed, her weakness to Marcus's sure touch was still there.

Her fingers entwined in the dark hair at his nape as he bent his head to capture one fiery-tipped breast between his lips, holding him to her, her head thrown back in pleasure, her breathing shallow and ragged.

But suddenly he was thrusting her away from him, a ruddy hue to his lean cheeks, his eyes the grey of slate. His mouth was twisted in contempt as he seemed almost to see her.

But of course he couldn't, he could have no idea of the abandonment in her face, the way her body still craved for his touch. But Olivia was very aware of it, and hastily pulled up her dress to fasten it over her nakedness, smoothing the material over her waist and hips with hands that still trembled.

Marcus thrust his hands through the dark thickness of his hair. 'So I got to grope my way over your body after all,' he rasped coldly.

Olivia swallowed hard. 'Marcus, I—'

'Strange,' he continued as if she hadn't spoken. 'You felt—familiar.'

She could feel the colour drain from her face. He couldn't possibly remember her! It had been six years, she had changed, matured. Heavens, if her name hadn't struck any memories how could he possibly remember her body! His wife had died three years ago, there had to have been a lot of women since then. They hadn't even made love, he *couldn't* have remembered her!

'Olivia?' he was frowning.

'I'm still here,' she told him jerkily.

'I know that,' he snapped harshly. 'I thought I'd just successfully proved that all my other senses function perfectly normally.'

Two bright wings of colour heightened her cheeks. 'You have—I mean, you did,' she fumbled over the words in her embarrassment. 'I just—I have to go down to dinner now. Your food will be—be cold, I'll bring you a fresh tray.'

'Strangely enough I'm no longer hungry,' he

drawled, mocking her. 'I think my appetite has just been satisfied.'

She swallowed hard, her breath catching in her throat at his insulting tone. 'Then you're easily pleased, Mr Hamilton,' she derided contemptuously. 'I feel far from satisfied myself. But then I can leave this prison to find someone to help me with that. Goodnight, Mr Hamilton.'

'You little——'

She left the room before his outstretched hands could reach her. He had looked murderous, as if he would like to put those hands around her throat—and slowly strangle her.

She leant weakly against the wall outside. What little progress she had made with Marcus today had been wiped out by those few hurtful words she had just hurled at him. Her only excuse was that he had been hurting her too, and she had needed to hit out in her defence. But that wasn't really an excuse at all; she was a nurse, Marcus was her patient, she should have had more control, should never have allowed herself to lose her temper in the way she had.

Was it possible that Marcus did still remember her, somehow in his subconscious mind know that he had touched her that way before? If he should ever remember just how and when he had touched her . . .! She would have no choice but to leave then. Six years ago she had loved Marcus, and he couldn't help but have known that. But he had made his choice, had chosen his wife, and for her to be here now, working with him as she was, would show him that the love she had thought dead long ago was still very much alive. Tonight, as he made love to her, as he kissed and touched her, had proved that she still loved Marcus Hamilton!

CHAPTER FIVE

SYBIL was at her most cutting during dinner, although Sally seemed unaware of it, and chattered happily throughout the meal, obviously more relaxed about her father now that Olivia was here to take care of him. Olivia just wished she could have the same confidence; she had no idea how she was going to face Marcus on a professional level after the way he had kissed her.

The housekeeper appeared in the doorway as they sat in the lounge drinking coffee. 'Telephone for you, Miss King,' she smiled.

Olivia frowned. 'For me? Are you sure?' She hadn't even written to tell her parents where she was yet, let alone anyone else.

'I'm sure, Miss King,' the housekeeper nodded.

Olivia followed Miss Podmore out into the hallway, sitting down in the chair there to take the call, absently watching the housekeeper as she went upstairs to collect Marcus's tray.

'Miss King?' an unfamiliar male voice queried at her softly spoken hello.

'Yes?' she replied in a puzzled voice.

'Simon Brooks here, Olivia,' he explained lightly. 'I may call you Olivia, I hope?'

A mental picture of the doctor came to mind, pleasantly attractive, charming too. 'Of course,' she acknowledged smoothly. 'I couldn't think who was calling me for a moment.'

'I'm not interrupting your dinner, am I?' he asked worriedly.

'Not at all,' she dismissed, relieved to have an

excuse to leave the tense atmosphere between herself and Sybil Carr, if only for a moment. 'I've already eaten.'

'So have I. Which is perhaps as well, because I— we—What I'm trying to say, and not very well,' he said self-derisively, 'is that I would like to see you tonight.'

'Oh.' Olivia swallowed hard. Simon Brooks might be all the things she had thought he was, but after the discovery of her love for Marcus, she really wasn't interested in dating another man. 'I—well——'

'I think we should talk about Marcus,' Simon added, sensing her discomfort.

'Of course,' she realised with relief. She and the doctor had had little opportunity to talk extensively about Marcus's long-term recovery, merely discussing the medication and the mental anguish he was suffering now. 'Where shall we meet?'

'I'll call for you,' he told her briskly. 'I'm leaving the hospital now, so I should be with you in about twenty minutes. Okay?'

'Fine,' she agreed.

'How are you bearing up after your first day?' Simon sounded amused.

'Exactly as you might have expected,' she said dryly. 'Barely.'

Simon laughed softly before ringing off. Olivia was still sitting in the hallway as Miss Podmore came down with the tray.

'How did he do?' She raised her brows.

'Not very well,' the housekeeper frowned. 'He asked for you, by the way.'

She stood up smoothly. 'I was just going up to him.' She went slowly up the stairs, not looking forward to facing Marcus again, not after what had happened between them earlier this evening. But she had stopped being shy little Olivia King long ago; she was a competent and successful nurse, and she had decided she would continue to treat Marcus as she would any other patient in her care.

The sight that met her eyes as she walked into the room banished any such thoughts. Marcus was just emerging from the adjoining bathroom, his hair still damp from the shower he had just taken, his only clothing a pair of black silk pyjama trousers that rested low down on his lean hips. Olivia stood transfixed in the doorway, her gaze drawn again and again to the wide expanse of his chest, to the dark wiry hair growing there, his shoulders broad and muscled, his stomach taut and flat.

He came to a halt as he sensed her presence in the room, his head tilted slightly to one side as he listened for any sign of movement. 'Who's there?' he barked.

She moistened her dry lips, intending to answer him, but finding difficulty doing so.

'Olivia,' he guessed scornfully, the tension leaving him as he moved confidently about the room. 'Well, come in, for God's sake!' he rasped as she still made no effort to move. 'I wouldn't want Miss Podmore to come back and be shocked.'

'Meaning I'm not?' she quietly closed the door behind her.

'I doubt it,' he drawled. 'I'm far from the first near-naked man you've ever seen.'

'No—I've nursed a lot of men during my training and since.'

'I wasn't referring to nursing them,' he mocked, moving to sit on the side of the bed. 'Where are you going?' he snapped as he heard her moving.

'To the bathroom,' she answered abruptly. 'It's time for your medication. Do you want sleeping pills too?' she paused at the door.

'Yes,' he bit out tersely, lying back on top of the bedclothes. 'What else is there to do but sleep?'

Olivia flinched at the dull bitterness in his voice, going into the bathroom to get his medication. His eyes were closed as she came back into the bedroom, although the lids were raised above intelligent grey eyes as he sat up to take the glass of water out of her hand.

He threw the tablets to the back of his throat, swallowing all the water before handing her back the glass. 'I thought you were going out?' he taunted, propped up by several pillows now.

'I am,' she replied with satisfaction, knowing by his dark frown that he hadn't expected that reply.

'Where?' he demanded to know.

Olivia stiffened at his arrogant tone. 'I haven't actually discussed my duties with Sally in detail yet, but I'm sure she intends for my evenings to be my own.'

'In other words, it's none of my business where you're going,' he bit out fiercely.

'Exactly.'

'Olivia——'

'Do you need anything else before I go out?' she asked briskly.

'I need a lot of things,' he stated coldly, his face averted from her. 'But I won't *ask* for any of them.'

She frowned at the defeat in his voice. 'I don't understand——'

'I don't suppose you do,' Marcus mocked. 'Why should you? Who is he, Olivia?' he demanded abruptly.

'He . . .?'

'The man who's going to help ease the frustration I caused,' he scorned.

She blushed as she remembered the claim she had made when he made her lose her temper. 'I don't——'

'Who, Olivia!'

She drew in an angry breath at the fury in his voice.

'Simon,' she told him almost defiantly. 'I'm going out with Simon Brooks.'

Marcus's scowl darkened. 'My assistant?'

'Yes.'

'I see. At least, I think I do,' he added slowly. 'Do you always get this—involved with the doctor concerned in your patient's case?'

His insults were really beginning to wound now, and she knew she had to get away from him, if only for a few hours. But she had no one else to blame but herself for this situation, had known exactly what was involved when she accepted this job, had known Marcus's antagonism towards her was part of his treatment. If only it weren't slowly destroying her!

'If the circumstances warrant it,' she managed to reply aloofly, preparing to leave.

'If he's good-looking enough, you mean,' Marcus taunted.

'Yes,' she snapped, 'that's exactly what I mean!'

His hand moved and his fingers closed about her wrist like a vice. 'Do you make a habit of sleeping with doctors?'

Olivia wrenched out of his grasp, two bright spots of colour in her cheeks as she walked over to the door. 'If I like them,' she replied angrily. 'Didn't you know nurses are notorious for sleeping with doctors?'

His mouth twisted. 'Mine never did.'

'Maybe you just chose the wrong nurses to ask!' She slammed out of the room, surprised to see her hands were shaking. What else would she do or say before this was over?

'Marcus isn't the easiest of men to understand, even when he's well,' Simon smiled his sympathy as they sat together in a secluded booth in a local pub.

'He certainly isn't!' Olivia hadn't calmed down yet, despite the fact that she and Simon had been in this comfortably relaxed saloon bar for the last ten minutes. She had spent all that time telling him how impossible Marcus had been today. Although she told him nothing about the incident just before dinner, that was too private, and illuminating, for anyone but herself and Marcus to know.

Simon shook his head. 'Sally told me you and Marcus knew each other before this.' He sounded puzzled.

'It was a long time ago,' she grimaced.

'Marcus has given no indication that he remembers you.'

'We weren't exactly friends!'

'Oh?'

'No,' she avoided his gaze.

'And yet you rushed to his bedside as soon as you heard about the accident.'

'Sally telephoned me——'

'Olivia,' Simon interrupted her softly, 'were you in love with Marcus in the past?'

'No! Yes,' she admitted huskily at his sceptical look. 'A long time ago I was. Why do you need to know?'

'I'm glad you realise I *need* to know,' he grimaced ruefully. 'I don't usually pry into the private feelings of people I barely know. But I need to know the extent of your own concern for Marcus.'

She blushed. 'Any nurse would be concerned. He's a brilliant surgeon——'

'I'm not interested in your feelings as a nurse, although that does enter into it,' Simon added with a frown. 'I take it you want what's best for Marcus?'

'But of course!' She sounded incredulous that he should need to ask.

'Even if his best and mine don't coincide?'

Her mouth twisted. 'If Marcus did what he wanted he would waste the rest of his life sitting in a chair by his bedroom window!'

Simon smiled, his brown eyes warm. 'Have you told him that?'

'Among other things,' she admitted ruefully. 'I warned you, we bring out the worst in each other.'

'The only times I've seen him in the least approaching the old dynamic Marcus was after you visited him at the hospital.'

'When he lost his temper,' she sighed.

'But at least then he was fighting back,' Simon pointed out softly.

She shrugged acknowledgment of that fact. 'So what else do you want me to do to help him?'

Simon sat forward eagerly. 'Jason Fitzgerald is coming over from America on Friday,' he mentioned the famous optic specialist with a casualness that deceived no one. 'To see Marcus.'

'But that's wonderful!' Olivia cried excitedly.

'No, it isn't.'

'Not——? Oh,' she chewed worriedly on her bottom lip. 'There's one person you have yet to tell, hm?' she grimaced.

'Exactly,' he sighed.

'And you want me to do it.'

'Oh, I could tell him,' Simon said lightly. 'Anyone could tell him. But I believe only one person could convince him to see Fitzgerald.'

'Me,' she realised flatly.

'Yes,' he confirmed.

'But I don't understand,' Olivia frowned her puzzlement. 'Marcus wants to see again. Surely he'll let Fitzgerald examine him if it's going to give him that chance?'

Simon sighed, shaking his head. 'Try to understand, Olivia. Marcus is an exceptional man, a genius in his field—and he's frightened.'

'Frightened . . .?' she echoed dazedly. Fear wasn't an emotion she connected with Marcus, although he had once proved to her very effectively that surgeons and doctors had feelings too. But what could he be afraid of?

'Wouldn't you be?' Simon's expression was intent. 'While he hides himself away in the house, while he refuses to see a specialist, he can tell himself that one day he'll see again, that it's only temporary.'

'But he seems so sure he's never going to see again!'

'No, he isn't,' Simon shook his head. 'Bitterness is just his best form of defence at the moment. If he sees Fitzgerald, and he tells him that the blindness is permanent, then he really will have no hope left. And he can't take that.'

'Then why put him through it?' she demanded to know. 'He's already been through enough. I won't be responsible for making him suffer any more!'

'And if there's a chance he can see?' Simon reasoned. 'It isn't my field, Olivia, and directly after the accident the nerves were too sensitive for a reliable diagnosis. The time is right now. Will you deny him the chance to see again, to go back to being the first-class surgeon that he is?'

'You know I won't,' she choked. 'But I won't be the cause of any more pain either.'

'Fitzgerald may be able to operate.'

She had heard of the famous specialist, knew his reputation, and if anyone could help Marcus then he could. But if he couldn't do anything for him ... 'Marcus already hates me,' she said dully. 'If I do this to him I may not be able to continue working with him, he may not let me.'

Simon touched her hand gently. 'Think about it, Olivia. You have until Thursday evening to break it to him. After that I'll have to talk to him.'

'You know he hasn't even been out of the house since he came home?'

'Yes.'

'Just getting him to go out would be an achievement,' she frowned, shaking her head. 'Getting him to see a specialist ... I don't think I could do it even if I tried.'

'All I'm asking is that you try.' Simon squeezed her hand. 'Now that's enough business for tonight, let's talk about something else. I'm a very interesting subject,' he told her teasingly.

His derisive conceit made her laugh—as it was meant to do—and for the next hour they discussed their respective careers, Olivia finding that she liked this young surgeon more and more as the evening progressed. He had a good sense of humour and a charming manner. He also had a great respect and liking for Marcus, tremendous admiration for him as a surgeon.

'The highlight of my career was becoming his assistant,' Simon told her somewhat bashfully. 'It's an honour to work for him.'

'But who is in charge there now?'

'Me—temporarily,' he stressed the last. 'As soon as Marcus is well enough to return I'll gladly step down.'

'And if he never is?' she voiced the question neither of them wanted to.

'I refuse to think in the negative,' Simon said briskly. 'I think one of us doing that is enough—and I mean Marcus, not you,' he added hastily. 'I can't begin to thank you for the difference you've made in him already.'

Olivia's mouth twisted ruefully. 'It's the first time I've improved a patient's condition by making him hate me. It doesn't do much for my ego as a nurse.'

'And as a woman?' he prompted gently.

'To Marcus I'm not a woman,' she avoided. 'I'm his tormentor.' And he had become hers too! Marcus enjoyed mocking her, took a perverted pleasure from tormenting her. And the way she had responded to him earlier this evening could have done little to improve that, had merely given him another weapon to use against her.

'I'm sorry,' Simon said with compassion. 'It can't be pleasant for you.'

'If it helps Marcus . . .'

'Oh, it will,' he nodded.

She looked at her wrist-watch, surprised to see how late it was. 'I have to get back,' she said with genuine regret; she had enjoyed Simon's company, had found him intelligent and charming. 'I'd like to check on Marcus,' she explained.

'Of course.' He rose easily to his feet, holding out her lightweight jacket for her to slip her arms into; she had discarded the halter-necked dress from dinner in favour of fitted brown trousers and blouse, her jacket a cream linen. 'I'll come in and see him myself on Thursday. Perhaps we could have dinner together that evening?'

'I'd like that,' she accepted lightly. 'Thank you.'

It was after eleven when she let herself into the house with the key Sally had given her; Marcus should have been asleep hours ago. There was a message from Sally on the hall table telling her that she and her grandmother had gone to bed, but that there was coffee made in the kitchen if she wanted it. After pouring away the coffee Olivia made her way slowly up the stairs.

A light still showed under Marcus's door, and she opened it quietly. He lay sprawled out on the bed, the bedclothes on the floor, the perpetual frown he had when awake erased in sleep. Olivia couldn't resist the impulse to stand at his bedside, able to feast her eyes on him without earning his derision. He was very pale in sleep, the scars he had acquired from the accident more livid, his cheeks lean, his mouth, the mouth that scorned her so cruelly, was partly open, as if waiting for a lover's kiss.

Olivia brought herself up with a start, knowing she was on dangerous ground. Since the early days of her training she had schooled herself to care for, and about, her patients, but never to become that emotionally involved again. With Marcus she was breaking all her own rules.

She gently smoothed the hair back from his brow, loving the clean, crispness of it beneath her fingertips. Tomorrow they would be back to hating each other, but for this moment she allowed her love for him to flow, allowed herself to indulge in a little day-dreaming where he loved her too. How wonderful if Marcus were her husband, if she could climb into this bed beside him and wake him in the most pleasurable way there is between a man and a woman.

'You can if you like,' he murmured suddenly, the grey eyes looking directly at her as he turned his head, making it hard to believe he couldn't see her.

Her hand moved away jerkily, deep colour flooding her cheeks. 'I just came in to see if you needed anything. I—I thought you were asleep.'

His mouth twisted as he raised himself up on the pillows, the skin on his chest dark. 'And do you usually *touch* your patients when they're asleep?' he taunted.

'Of course not!'

'Did Simon prove unsatisfactory?' he demanded harshly. 'What a pity! Well my invitation still stands.'

Olivia swallowed hard, her hand selfconsciously at her throat. 'What invitation?'

'The one I just made for you to share my bed. Once you're here beside me I won't even be at a disadvantage.'

'You've never been at a disadvantage, Marcus,' she snapped. 'Neither now or——' she broke off selfconsciously.

His expression was suddenly intent. 'Or?' he prompted softly.

'You have a wonderful reputation as a surgeon,' she

compromised. 'Simon has been singing your praises all evening.'

'Indeed?' he drawled.

'Oh yes. He——'

'I'm not really interested in Simon, Olivia.'

'He said he would call in and see you Thursday evening,' she finished determinedly.

'I don't intend going anywhere!' he rasped.

Olivia flushed. 'God, your self-pity infuriates me!'

'Then leave,' he suggested coldly.

'I can't—and you know damn well I can't.'

'Do I?' he taunted.

'Yes,' she said fiercely. 'And you won't force me into it either. You might try, might even threaten me sexually——'

'What threat could a blind man be to you, sexually or otherwise?' Marcus taunted bitterly.

Her hands clenched into fists at her sides. 'You really want to know?'

'I wouldn't have asked otherwise,' he nodded.

Olivia moved to the door, her hand going to the light switch, plunging the room into darkness with a movement of her finger.

'What the—Did you just turn off the light?' Marcus demanded.

'Yes. Ouch!' she cursed as she walked into something. 'Well, you might help me,' she told him crossly. 'I'm completly lost, you know.'

'Then turn the light back on,' he said unconcernedly.

'I can't, I don't know where it is!' She was fumbling about in the dark, trying to remember what furniture stood in her way of getting to Marcus's bed. She remembered the chair, but unfortunately she forgot the footstool in front of it and landed in an untidy heap on the floor.

'Olivia!' Marcus cried his alarm at the sound of the heavy thump. 'What's happened?'

'I fell over,' she grumbled, trying to extricate herself from the footstool her legs had become entangled with. 'Oh, damn!' she muttered at the mess she had made over this simple lesson in psychology, in showing him that he was right, once they were in bed together he would be at no disadvantage.

'Olivia!' Firm hands grasped her arms as Marcus helped her to her feet. 'Are you all right?'

'Yes.' Her voice was husky at his proximity.

'What were you trying to prove?'

'I wasn't trying to prove anything,' she said crossly. 'I was just showing you that with the light out we're equal.'

'I think all you did was show me that in the dark I have an advantage over you,' he jeered. 'I knew exactly where you were in this room, you didn't have the faintest idea.'

'I still don't,' she muttered, her sanity returning. How far would she have been prepared to go to show Marcus that as a man he was still devastating? Her mind baulked from giving her an answer to that question.

'Here,' he guided her slowly across the room, one of his hands moving up to switch on the light. 'Feel better now?' he mocked.

She did, but she wasn't going to admit it. 'I'd better get to bed, it's late,' she said abruptly, very much aware of his near-nakedness.

'My offer is still open,' he drawled. 'And you can even leave the light on. It's been too long, Olivia,' he added throatily. 'I need a woman.'

If only he had phrased that differently, if only he had said it was *her* he needed! But he hadn't, and she felt her outrage was justified. 'How dare you!' she gasped. 'I'm your nurse, Mr Hamilton, nothing more.'

'You save everything else for the doctor involved, hmm?' he rasped.

She didn't even return that insult with an answer, quietly leaving the room. She heard him call her name as she closed the door, but she kept right on walking.

Even if she had given in to the impulse to share his bed she wouldn't have been Olivia to him, she would just have been a woman's body he could lose himself in for a while. How she hated him for reducing her love for him to that level!

If Olivia had expected that night-time visit to Marcus's room to have changed their relationship, for the best or for the worse, then she was wrong. Marcus seemed to have forgotten it, as cold and bitter as usual the next day, again refusing to accompany her down to the garden, in fact he still refused to leave his room at all.

'You're behaving like a child,' she snapped.

'I feel like one! I feel as if Sally is the responsible parent and I'm the child to be led about by the hand.' He turned away, a pulse beating erratically in his jaw. 'Do you have any idea what that can do to a man?'

'Oh, Marcus——'

'Get out of here!' he ordered through gritted teeth, his back turned towards her.

'Marcus——'

'Don't you understand, I need to be alone!' He wrenched his arm away from the hand she had put out to comfort him. 'Go down to the garden and keep Jasper company.'

She could sense his near-desperation, knew his real need to be alone. Most of her patients had times like these, and she respected Marcus's request as she would have done theirs, doing as he asked and going down to the garden.

The Labrador greeted her eagerly, and once again she spent the time playing with him. At five years old the dog had a lot of energy to use up, and Olivia was the one to drop down with exhaustion, deciding the quiet relaxation of reading Marcus the newspaper was what was called for now.

In fact they fell into an uneasy routine the next few days, uneasy because Marcus's mood was still explosive, his anger with the restrictions his blindness put on him seeming to increase by the day, coming to the point where she daren't even talk about it.

Consequently she hadn't been able to mention Jason Fitzgerald's visit to him; she hadn't been able to find the right moment. By Thursday afternoon she was getting desperate, knowing that Simon was depending on her. Sally had high hopes from the specialist's visit too. Olivia had tried to prepare the girl for the worst, but Sally remained optimistic. It was a feeling that was infectious, and it finally gave Olivia the courage to approach Marcus with the idea of going to the hospital the next day.

She finished the daily routine of reading the newspaper to him, lingering when she should have been going to get their tea.

'Well?' he barked, sensing her hesitation.

Olivia took a few seconds to study him, knowing it was increasing his impatience with her. But this last week Marcus had lost most of his unhealthy pallor, his increased appetite and the fresh air he got from the open window giving him a more healthy look. There was a leashed energy about his movements too now, and she knew that physically he would soon be beyond her care. What would happen to him then? She knew he enjoyed their verbal sparring, knew it by the light of challenge in his eyes as he shouted and raged at her, and if she were honest she knew she would miss their arguments too. She would miss Marcus . . .

Her love for him had increased the last few days, telling her that it had never really died, that it had only been buried beneath her disillusionment and pain at the callous way he had dropped her to return to his wife. If he hadn't gone back to Ruth—But he had, and he didn't even remember her now!

'Marcus, what do you know of Jason Fitzgerald?' If she had learnt one thing about him the last few days it was that he would accept only complete honesty, couldn't abide pretence of any kind.

He had stiffened at the mention of the specialist's name, paling slightly. 'What should I know?' he asked warily.

'Marcus——'

'What should I know, Olivia?' He stood up forcefully.

'Simon——'

'No!' Marcus rasped, glaring down at her, his expression fierce. 'I won't have the two of you plotting behind my back——'

'You're becoming paranoid!'

'Am I? Am I really?' he scorned. 'Do you deny that you and Simon have decided between the two of you that I should see Fitzgerald—without even consulting me?'

'Well, I——'

'Treating me like I'm a damned mental cabbage,' he muttered grimly, his face tense. 'The accident didn't affect my brain, Olivia, only my sight. You had no right to make such a decision for me!'

'But if we had asked you——'

'I would have said no,' he bit out predictably. 'As I am now.'

Olivia gasped at his implacability. 'But he's coming all the way from America just to see you!'

'Then he's had a wasted journey.' Marcus's mouth was twisted with bitterness. 'Because I have no intention of seeing him, either now or in the future!'

Her expression became pleading. 'Marcus——'

'The answer is no, Olivia,' he told her through gritted teeth.

'If you won't see him for your own sake then think of Sally,' she told him angrily. 'She's depending on this examination.'

Angry colour darkened his cheeks. 'You had no right to raise her hopes before asking me!'

'I had confidence in your intelligence——'

'Then you shouldn't have done! I won't see Fitzgerald or anyone else.' He turned away from her, his back rigid with tension.

'Marcus, listen to me!' She put her hand on his arm, and felt the way he flinched at her touch. Her hand slowly dropped back to her side. 'I know you're frightened, but——'

'Frightened?' His savagery as he spun round made her shrink back. 'I'm not *frightened*, I'm just sick of idiots like you telling me what's best for me. What do you know about being blind? What do you know of my feelings?' His hands were clenched into fists, almost as if he would like to strike her. 'You know *nothing*! And I want you out of my house, *tonight*, do you hear?'

'I hear,' she confirmed dully.

'Then make sure you leave.' He turned away again. 'Tonight,' he repeated coldly. 'And tell Simon I won't see Fitzgerald. Or any other specialists he cares to consult.'

'Jason Fitzgerald is the best there is, and you know it,' she choked.

Marcus didn't even answer her, and Olivia had no choice but to leave the room, leaning weakly back against the door. Marcus had meant it, he definitely wanted her out of his house. And she didn't want to go, she couldn't leave him, not when she loved him so much.

CHAPTER SIX

'Whew!' Sally ran up the remainder of the stairs she had been ascending as Olivia came out of Marcus's bedroom. 'Dad's in fine voice today,' she grimaced.

Olivia schooled her features into cool calmness, unwilling to let Sally see just how upset she had been by this last argument with Marcus. 'I didn't see you there,' she smiled. 'And yes, your father is in a fighting mood.'

Sally gave another grimace. 'He didn't like the idea of seeing Mr Fitzgerald, I take it?'

'No.' Olivia searched the younger girl's face, trying to ascertain just how much of the heated conversation she had actually heard. She didn't look too disturbed, so she probably hadn't heard much at all. 'In fact, he's refused to do so.'

'I thought as much,' Sally sighed. 'I couldn't hear what was being said, just the raised voices. I'll talk to him.'

'I shouldn't.' Olivia stopped the other girl with her hand on the door-handle, lowering her voice, remembering that Marcus could hear them through the closed door. 'Not yet anyway,' she soothed at Sally's frown. 'Give him a little time to think it over. Why not go down and ask Miss Podmore for some tea, and then talk to him when you take it in to him?' Perhaps by that time Marcus would have calmed down. Although she doubted it; he had seemed adamant in his decision. But she would leave it to him to tell Sally he had ordered her to leave, he couldn't evade the responsibility for his actions.

'Okay,' Sally agreed eagerly to her suggestion.

During the other girl's absence in the kitchen Olivia telephoned Simon at the hospital and told him exactly what had happened.

'Never mind,' he comforted. 'I'll talk to him myself this evening. I'll make it early, then he can have the rest of the evening to think about it.'

'There's something else.' She chewed worriedly on her bottom lip. 'He's told me to leave, and this time I think he meant it.'

'Hm,' Simon sighed. 'Well, don't do anything about it yet. Stay away from him and give him a chance to calm down.'

'And if he doesn't change his mind?'

'He will. He has to,' Simon added firmly. 'You're the best thing to happen to him. He has to be intelligent enough to realise that.'

Marcus gave no evidence of backing down from his decision, and when the time came for his early evening medication Olivia instructed Sally what to give him. Sally had told her that her father was still determined not to see Jason Fitzgerald, although he was calmer about it now. The last thing he needed was for Olivia to put in an appearance and upset him again!

And so she stayed away from him, his lack of curiosity as to her whereabouts telling her that he had assumed she had already left his house and his employ. She knew that she was being blamed unfairly for something that could, in the end, be Marcus's salvation, but he was in no mood to understand that right now. As far as Marcus was concerned she and Simon had deceived him, and that was unforgivable.

Simon arrived at seven-thirty, very handsome in a dark suit and light blue shirt. Olivia took him through to the lounge, all the time conscious of Sybil Carr's speculative looks as she and Sally had a pre-dinner drink.

'I may as well go straight up and see Marcus,'

Simon said briskly after polite greetings had been made. 'I think I know what's involved.'

'Good luck!' Olivia grimaced.

'I think I'll probably need it,' he nodded ruefully.

'I've had no joy with him at all,' Sally told Olivia once the young surgeon had gone upstairs. 'He refuses to even talk about it. In fact,' she frowned, 'he isn't talking much at all.'

'Because he knows a specialist is unnecessary,' Sybil put in coldly. 'Or a nurse either, for that matter.' Her gaze passed insultingly over Olivia. 'He just needs to be left alone.'

'To do what?' Olivia challenged. The other woman's manner angered her.

'Why, to get well again, of course,' Sybil derided.

'And just how is he going to do that without professional help?' she snapped.

'Your sort of professional help he doesn't need!'

'Grandmother!' Sally gasped her surprise at the insult.

'If you'll both excuse me I think I'll go and finish getting ready for my dinner date,' Olivia said coldly. 'I wouldn't want to keep Simon waiting,' she taunted the older woman.

The blue eyes hardened questioningly. 'You're going out with Mr Brooks?'

'Yes,' she replied haughtily, 'I am. And I don't want to delay our leaving.' She swept out of the room.

Sybil Carr really was the most bitchily insulting woman she had ever met! Her innuendoes and insults made an already difficult job almost impossible. If it weren't for the fact that Olivia genuinely believed she was doing Marcus some good as his nurse she would leave here tonight and never come back. She might have to do that anyway if Marcus didn't change his mind. Despite what she had told him when she first came here, she couldn't stay against his will.

She was waiting downstairs in the small sitting-room when Simon came back downstairs half an hour later, standing up at his entrance, tall and slender in an emerald-coloured dress that reached just below her knees, her hair a fluffy red-gold cloud about her shoulders.

Simon's eyes darkened appreciatively, the strain he had been under while with Marcus leaving him as he smiled warmly at her. 'You look beautiful,' he told her huskily, bending down to kiss her lightly on the lips.

She was a little taken aback at the intimacy, especially as it had been uninvited. But she returned the light gesture, feeling in need of a little affection herself after being at the brunt of Marcus's caustic tongue this past week.

'Olivia, I—Oh!' Sally came to an abrupt halt in the doorway, a high flush to her cheeks. 'I didn't mean to—to interrupt,' she stumbled over her words in her embarrassment.

'You didn't.' Simon turned, his arm still about Olivia's shoulders. 'We've both had run-ins with your father today, and we were just comforting each other.' He made light of what had, after all, been only a platonic kiss, no passion existing on either side.

Sally grinned mischievously. 'I had one too, so do I merit a kiss?' She raised one dark brow questioningly.

Olivia could sense Simon's indecision, then he shrugged, his arm falling away from her shoulders as he moved to kiss Sally on the lips. 'Okay?' he murmured softly.

'Er—yes.' For a moment Sally looked disconcerted, and then she bounced back with her usual good humour. 'My first grown-up kiss!' she mocked Simon's first hesitation.

He laughed at the taunt. 'You'll get more than you bargained for if you don't behave yourself,' he threatened softly.

She gave him an impudent grin. 'Just say the word . . .!' She turned to Olivia. 'I wanted to apologise for my grandmother's behaviour. She's been acting very strangely since Daddy's accident,' she frowned.

'She's been under a lot of strain, Sally,' she dismissed with more sincerity than she felt. 'I don't take any notice of her barbs.'

'Well, if you're sure . . .?'

'I am,' she smiled, not wanting to upset Sally. 'Now go and have your dinner before it gets cold.'

'What was all that about?' Simon asked as he drove them to the restaurant.

'Nothing important,' she shrugged. 'Mrs Carr doesn't particularly like me in the house. But then she wouldn't like any nurse there.' She wasn't sure that was the truth; Sybil Carr's insults were highly personal for the main part. 'She doesn't think Marcus needs one.'

Simon frowned. 'I don't remember Anna having any trouble with her.'

'Then maybe it's just me she doesn't like,' Olivia dismissed lightly. 'I'm not worried about it, so I don't think anyone else should be either.'

'If you say so,' but he didn't sound convinced.

'How did you get on with Marcus?' She decided it would be best to change the subject.

He heaved a deep sigh. 'Not very well. Let's talk about it over dinner, shall we?'

She nodded, seeing that he was as worried about getting Marcus to see Jason Fitzgerald as she was.

'He refused, of course,' Simon told her as they ate their meal in the quietly intimate restaurant, where the atmosphere was conducive to conversation. 'But then I knew he would,' he shrugged.

'You did?'

'Oh yes,' he nodded, 'I think I would too in his place, in fact I'm sure I would. No news is good news as far as he's concerned. But I've given him something to think about,' he added with satisfaction. 'Fitzgerald has fitted this visit to England in between a very tight schedule, a schedule that doesn't leave him free again for six months. If Marcus turns down this opportunity I don't know when Jason will be able to see him again.'

'You told Marcus that?'

'Yes.'

'What was his reaction?'

'No interest,' Simon grimaced. 'But he has another sixteen hours to think about it. The appointment is for two o'clock. I think it would be better if you drove him to the—You can drive, can't you?'

'Yes,' she laughed. 'But if he changes his mind and agrees to go I'd willingly carry him there! You really think this time alone will convince him?' Her humour faded.

'If it doesn't we've failed.'

'I've already done that,' she told him softly. 'If Marcus goes to the hospital tomorrow it will be all your doing.'

'If—that's the real question,' he frowned. 'How do you think Sally is bearing up under the strain of all this?' he asked suddenly.

Olivia looked at him from beneath lowered lashes. 'Very maturely.' She knew by the instant flush to his cheeks that she had been right in her earlier surmise; Simon was more than a little interested in Sally, as she sensed the girl was more than a little interested in him.

'She likes to tease me,' he said ruefully. 'That kiss, for instance.'

'*That* was teasing?' she mocked gently.

'Of course.' His face hardened, as if he were angry with himself for even mentioning it. 'Sally is a child.'

Her expression softened sympathetically. 'A woman of eighteen is as capable of falling in love as one of twenty-five. I know, I did it myself,' she added softly.

Simon looked despondent. 'But it wasn't the sort of love that lasted, was it.'

'Yes—yes, it was.'

He gave her a searching look, realisation dawning at the steady glow of love in her face. 'I had no idea . . .' he groaned. 'I imagined you'd got over what you and Marcus had.'

'What *I* had,' she corrected. 'Marcus had no idea that I ever loved him.'

'Then being with him now must be hell for you.'

'No more than your believing Sally is still a child. Believe me,' she touched his hands, 'she isn't.'

'Maybe when all this is over——'

'If it ever is. It's a possibility that has to be faced,' she realised heavily.

'Not yet, not until after Marcus has seen Fitzgerald.'

Her eyes were wide. 'You sound pretty confident that he will see him.'

'Wishful thinking,' Simon grimaced. 'But that's enough about work for now. Tell me about Olivia King,' he smiled encouragingly.

Olivia laughed softly. 'Only if you'll tell me about Simon Brooks.'

'Deal!' he grinned.

It was a pleasant evening, made the more so because both of them knew they met only as friends, colleagues, that both their romantic interests lay elsewhere.

From dinner they went on to a club, dancing together until after twelve, when Olivia decided she really should get back. She had left instructions with Sally about Marcus's medication, nevertheless she wanted to check on him before she herself went to bed; she had made that a nightly ritual.

'I'll see you tomorrow,' Simon smiled as he left her at the door.

'You hope,' she warned before quietly letting herself into the house.

Everyone had gone to bed, but that wasn't really surprising, it was almost one o'clock in the morning. There was no note from Sally tonight, but she checked that there was no coffee in the kitchen anyway, delaying the moment when she would have to go to Marcus's room. She felt nervous about seeing him again, even when he was asleep.

But finally she couldn't delay any longer, not surprised to see the light showing under his door; it was left on most nights. But she sensed that tonight it was different; she knew it as soon as she opened the door. Instead of being sprawled on the bed as he usually was Marcus sat in the armchair in front of the window, still fully dressed, the curtains drawn against the night as he faced only the brown velvet.

He turned sharply as Olivia closed the door, frowning, his head slightly tilted to one side in puzzlement, his features harshly defined, his expression fierce.

She hadn't dreamt he would still be out of bed, let alone that he would be awake too! Another confrontation between them was the last thing he needed. 'I'm sorry, Marcus, I thought—I thought you would be asleep,' she finished lamely.

Instead of the angry tirade she had been expecting he gave a choked sound, his hands tightly grasping the chair. 'I thought you'd gone!'

She put out her hands appealingly, then dropped them back to her sides as she realised he couldn't see her. 'I won't do that, Marcus,' she told him dully. 'No matter how many times you tell me to go.'

He frowned. 'Sally said you'd left the house.'

'I did. I've been out for the evening,' she revealed reluctantly.

'With Simon?' he rasped. 'Don't bother to deny it,'

his mouth twisted. 'I can smell his aftershave on you!
It's very potent, Olivia—is the man as effective?'

'Marcus!' she gasped her dismay.

'Is he?' His hand came out to grasp her wrist. 'Tell
me!'

'I'm not telling you anything!' She wrenched away
from him, rubbing her bruised wrist. 'I came in here
to see if you're all right—I can see that you are.
Goodnight!'and she hurried from the room before she
said anything to make matters worse.

She could hear him moving restlessly about the next
room as she lay in her bed, knew of his disturbed
thoughts as he paced the floor minute after minute,
hour after hour. She wanted to go to him, wanted to
comfort him, to help him through this. But she knew
he wouldn't welcome her understanding, that she was
the last person he wanted around him in his emotional
torment. But she couldn't stand his pacing, was aware
of his every move, finally pulling her pillow over her
head to block out the sound of his movements. He
couldn't go on like that all night, if he finally did
decide to see Jason Fitzgerald he wouldn't be fit
enough for the examination. And neither would she!

'Olivia?'

She froze in the bed, slowly removing the pillow
from her head. In the gloom of the room she could
clearly see Marcus standing beside the bed. In that
moment she could think only of the fact that Marcus
had left his bedroom, that he had finally made the
effort to leave the room that had become his prison.

'Olivia!' he rasped again, more uncertainly this time.

'I'm here,' she told him huskily, swinging her legs to
the floor as she sat up in front of him. 'I'm here,
Marcus.' She clasped his hands in hers as she looked
up at him.

'I need you,' he stated simply.

'Need . . .?' She swallowed hard.

'I need to be with you, to be held by you. I just need to be with you,' he finished in a tortured voice. 'Is that asking too much?'

He looked so vulnerable standing rigidly in the moonlight, shadows cast over his harsh face, and there was no thought of denial in her mind—or her heart. 'No,' she said huskily, 'that isn't asking too much.'

'Will Simon mind?' he sneered in the face of his deep need.

'Marcus——'

'Forget I said that!' He turned away. 'Forget I ever came here. It was a mistake. I just—I thought you'd really gone earlier——' He ran a hand across his face in a weary gesture.

'I'm here, Marcus,' Olivia repeated reassuringly, and stood up, her arms going about his waist from behind, her hands moving up his chest as she leant her cheek against the rigidity of his firm back. 'And I'm going to stay here. Come to bed and let me—let me hold you.' She could feel the tension in his body, his breathing ragged.

'You're sure?' he ground out.

'Very,' she answered without reserve.

Marcus turned with a heartfelt sigh, his arms like steel bands about her. 'I'll see Fitzgerald,' he rasped harshly, his face buried in her scented hair as he trembled against her.

'You will?' she cried excitedly, looking up into his grim face.

'I will,' he confirmed abruptly. 'But he's the last one. If he says there's no chance then that's it. Agreed?'

'Marcus——'

'I said no more, Olivia. Do you agree?' he demanded hardly.

She chewed her bottom lip. Jason Fitzgerald was the top man in his field, and if he said Marcus would never see again then that was probably final. But there was always that lingering doubt. Could she make such a promise and keep to it?

'I mean it, Olivia,' Marcus bit out at her hesitation. 'There will be no more specialists, no more tests.'

'All right,' she agreed with a deep sigh, knowing he was implacable. 'Let me help you,' she offered as he began to unbutton his shirt. Marcus was a man who needed no one, and the fact that he had come to her filled her with gratitude.

'All right.' His hands dropped to his sides.

Her hands trembled as she unbuttoned the rest of his shirt and stripped it from his shoulders, his skin deeply bronzed in the moonlight. He stood motionless as she released the catch to his trousers and slipped them down his legs, his only clothing now a pair of black underpants.

'No!' his hand stilled hers as she would have removed those too. 'That's enough. Just show me where the bed is,' he requested wearily.

She held his hand as she guided him into the bed. 'It's only a single,' she frowned as he lay down. 'Maybe we should use your room?'

'No,' he held out his hands for her to join him. 'This will do just fine.'

Olivia looked down at him with all the love inside her, then she slid into the bed beside him, knowing she would go to this man whenever he needed her. The fact that she would just be another female body to him didn't matter; he *needed* her.

His arms came about her and pulled her close in the confines of the bed, resting his hand against her silk-covered breasts with a ragged sigh of satisfaction. 'I'm so tired, Olivia. So very tired,' he told her weakly.

His legs were entwined with hers, his body pressed intimately against hers, and yet within minutes, by the deep and even tenor of his breathing, she knew he was fast asleep!

Her main emotion was disappointment. She had thought when he said he needed her that . . . God, she had *wanted* him to make love to her, had thought that was what he needed—and what she surely needed too! It was torture to lie beside him like this when her hands ached to caress him, to arouse him to the heights of passion, to know his full and absolute possession.

Marcus moved restlessly in his sleep, and in the narrow width of the bed each movement was exquisite torture to Olivia as she lay awake beside him hour after hour, needing to sleep but needing Marcus more. She felt like a wanton as she finally gave in to the temptation to caress and touch his body, loving the firm feel of his flesh, the warmth of his skin, his masculine beauty.

As her caresses became bolder, more intimate, he rolled away from her, pushing her hands away with a groan of protest. 'I don't want you, can't you understand that,' he muttered in his sleep. 'Ruth! Don't go, for God's sake don't leave me again. I love you, I've always loved you.' He was becoming more and more agitated. 'Olivia, no! Why did you leave me? Oh God, why did you leave me?' he cried out his pain.

It seemed that only when he was asleep, in his subconscious, could Marcus remember that he had once known a little nurse called Olivia King, a young girl who had merely been a diversion to him, while Ruth was the woman he really loved.

'Marcus!' She had to wake him, he was beginning to shout, he would wake the whole household. And the last thing they needed was for him to be found in her bed. 'Marcus, it's all right!' She shook him slightly as he seemed to be in a deep sleep.

'What the——' The long dark lashes were raised as

he woke up. 'Where am I?' he asked raggedly. 'Who are you?' he demanded as he felt the softness of the female body beside him. 'Olivia . . .?' he questioned uncertainly.

'Yes,' she confirmed. 'You were having a—a nightmare.' Her voice shook at the wealth of love Marcus still had for Ruth. And she had thought he had come in here to make love to her! 'You were shouting,' she calmed him.

'I'm sorry.' He ran a hand over his eyes. 'Is it still night?'

'Yes. You've only been asleep a couple of hours.' Her voice was low.

His arms tightened about her. 'Olivia . . .!' His mouth covered hers in rough demand.

Olivia knew that she should deny him. He still loved his wife, would always love her even though she was dead. But as his body hardened against hers she was unable to move away from him.

'You feel so soft,' he murmured against her shoulder. 'Like silk,' he added throatily, gently pushing the ribbon straps of her nightgown down her arms, baring her breasts to his searching lips, capturing one taut nipple to caress it with his tongue and teeth, tugging gently on the sensitive nub until its twin ached for the same pleasure.

His hand moved surely to feel her rising excitement, caressing the moist nipple his lips had just left, while his mouth moved to the other rosy peak, satisfying its hunger with a thoroughness that had her arching her body against his, her hips moving restlessly in erotic need. With deft hands Marcus removed her nightgown altogether, his dark underpants quickly following, and all thought of Ruth, of the love Marcus still had for the other woman, fled as their naked bodies became entwined, Marcus's thighs throbbing with desire.

They clung together damply as the desire grew to

frightening proportions, and Olivia gasped as Marcus kissed her inner thigh, till she cried out with pleasure.

'Have there been many lovers, Olivia?' His lips returned to her mouth, his breath warm on her face.

Olivia was still lost in the euphoric glow of the pleasure he had so easily created, looking up at him dazedly. 'I don't——'

'Have there?' he demanded, shaking her slightly, above her in the moonlight. 'Your body reacts too quickly and satisfyingly for you to be a novice.'

She stiffened at the insult. 'Marcus——'

'I need to know,' he ground out. 'Don't you understand?'

'Why do you need to know?' Passion was fading fast in the face of his insistence. 'Do you want to know the strength of your competition?'

'No,' he groaned, 'it isn't that.'

'Then what is it?' She moved completely away from him, getting out of bed to pick up her pale green nightgown from the floor, pulling it on over her nakedness, feeling more confident with its protective covering, despite the fact that Marcus couldn't see her. She looked down at him, the man on the bed unable to see her aroused loveliness, the drugging sensuality of her eyes. 'Why do you need to know, Marcus?' she demanded. 'I've asked nothing of you. Nothing!'

'Then perhaps you should have,' he snapped grimly, unconcerned with his own nakedness.

'What do you want me to do, ask for a list of the women you've slept with since your wife died?'

His mouth twisted. 'It wouldn't be much of a list.'

No, of course it wouldn't. Loving his wife as he did, Marcus wouldn't want to make love to anyone else. He was a sensual man, she had always known that, but it was a sensuality he could control. She doubted there had been any women for him since Ruth.

'I'm sorry,' she said dully, moving away.

'Where are you going?' he rasped.

'To get some hot milk,' she told him jerkily. 'I would appreciate it if you would be gone by the time I get back.'

'Olivia——'

'Please, Marcus!' Her voice broke with the strain she was under. 'I realise that what happened just now makes me look completely selfish, that you didn't— well, I'm sorry that I—and you didn't.' She stopped before the conversation became too embarrassing, never having completely lost control before, embarrassed at the shuddering response Marcus had induced in her. 'I want you to go. And don't—don't ever come in here again. I don't provide those sort of services!' She was blinded so badly by her tears that she could hardly see where she was going, stumbling out of the door and down the stairs to the kitchen.

She didn't really want the hot milk, and yet she prepared it anyway, relieved to have something to do. Although the task didn't occupy her mind, her thoughts were all too self-condemning. She had been a fool to respond to him so freely, had allowed herself to be betrayed by her own love, all the time knowing Marcus didn't return her feelings.

He had gone by the time she returned to her room, and unable to fight the emotion any longer, she sat down on the bed and sobbed out her pain.

It was late when she woke the next morning, and after a hurried shower she dressed in a blue and red patterned skirt and navy blue tee-shirt, going down to the kitchen to get a cup of coffee before she had to face Marcus, her embarrassment about last night, her uninhibited response, still acute.

'Have some breakfast too,' Miss Podmore insisted warmly.

'At ten-thirty it's almost lunch-time!' Olivia grimaced, surprised that no one had woken her. Although Marcus was probably no more eager for them to meet again than she was. 'I'll wait, thanks. I have to get back up to Mr Hamilton,' she smiled to hide her lack of confidence about the meeting.

'He isn't upstairs,' the housekeeper told her with a shake of her head.

'He isn't?' Olivia frowned.

'He's in the garden. He had breakfast out there this morning.'

She could hardly believe it; Marcus had made yet another move to break out of his self-imposed prison! 'I—How did he get downstairs?' she asked.

'He just walked down on his own—with a lot of swearing,' Miss Podmore added disapprovingly, a small bustling woman who was easily shocked. 'I think he knocked his shins a few times,' she confided. 'It was the shock of my life when he walked in here and demanded his breakfast!'

'I can imagine.' Olivia could too, although she couldn't possibly guess what had brought about this change in Marcus. She hurriedly swallowed the last of her coffee. 'I'll go out to him now.'

The sun was shining brightly in the secluded garden, and Marcus was seated under the shade of a gaily-coloured sun-umbrella, a glass of lemonade on the table beside him. Jasper became aware of her presence first, getting up from his position at Marcus's feet to bound over and give her an ecstatic greeting; she and the Labrador had become good friends in the last few days.

Marcus turned in her direction as the dog gave excited barks, the dark glasses he wore hiding a lot of his face, and in turn a lot of his thoughts. 'Olivia?' he questioned softly.

Hot colour flooded her cheeks as she remembered

the magic of those firm sensual lips. 'Yes,' she confirmed huskily, patting the dog absently as he stayed at her side.

'Come and sit down,' he invited.

She did so, sitting on the edge of her chair opposite him, Jasper nudging at her hand.

'He wants the biscuit you usually bring him,' Marcus drawled.

Olivia flushed. 'How did you know . . .?'

'He nudged my hand for one when I came out here,' he explained derisively.

'Oh.' She chewed on her bottom lip, her embarrassment making it hard for her to talk to him.

Marcus seemed to sense her confusion. 'About last night,' he said suddenly. 'I want to say I'm sorry.'

'That's all right. I—It was my own fault. I shouldn't have——'

'You don't understand,' he rasped impatiently. 'I'm not sorry for what happened, I'm sorry I pried into your personal life and broke the mood.'

She swallowed hard. 'I see.'

'I doubt it,' his mouth twisted. 'And I'm not in a position to tell you. I may never be,' he added with bitterness.

Olivia frowned at his vehemence. 'I don't understand.'

'And I don't want you to.' He stood up jerkily. 'Would you take me up to my room now, I'd like to lie down for a while. I had a—a disturbed night,' he added tauntingly.

'Of course.' She put his hand in the crook of her arm, giving him soft decisive instructions as they went into the house and up the stairs. 'Do you want me to stay with you?' she asked quietly as he sat back in the chair with his eyes closed, the dark glasses discarded now he was once again in the house.

'No,' he replied abruptly. 'I'll see you at two o'clock.'

'Your lunch——'

'Not today, Olivia,' he bit out tautly.

She respected his wish to be alone, knowing how genuinely disturbed he was by the thought of going to the hospital. She was disturbed herself, remembering her promise to him last night. So much depended on Marcus's meeting with Jason Fitzgerald this afternoon.

This unexpected time alone gave her time for thought when she would really rather not have had any time at all! Marcus's apology, especially the nature of it, had come as a surprise. He really had wanted to make love to her, would have done so if his curiosity about her past hadn't got the better of him.

Did he remember her? Could he possibly have realised she was the gullible little first-year nurse she had known six years ago? He had given no indication that he knew that, and yet she felt an uneasiness. Six years ago he must have known of her infatuation with him; what construction would he put on her actions of last night if he ever realised she was the same girl?

He sat rigidly at her side as they drove to the hospital later that afternoon, disinclined to talk, his expression stony. Olivia had learnt from Miss Podmore that Marcus had insisted Sally go to college today rather than accompany him, and while she knew the young girl must have put up an argument, she had obeyed her father in this. She could understand his reluctance to have his daughter with him; if the examination proved to be negative then at least Sally wouldn't have to witness her father's desolation until the worst of it was over, and if it was positive then there would be plenty of time for celebration this evening. Whatever the result, it would be better if Sally didn't witness her father's reaction, not when he already felt so vulnerable.

Simon met them outside the main hospital doors,

shaking Marcus warmly by the hand, giving Olivia's shoulder a reassuring squeeze.

Several people greeted Marcus as they made their way to the consulting-room, and Olivia could see his tension rising with each step they took.

'I want you to wait here,' he instructed Olivia as they stood in the waiting area.

She glanced at Simon, seeing his frown. 'Oh, but——'

'I said wait here!' Marcus bit out forcefully, his agitation evident from his clenched fists at his sides.

She swallowed hard at his vehemence. 'All right,' she choked her agreement.

'Marcus, I really think——'

'Do you imagine I want a witness to this?' Marcus ground out savagely, glaring in the other man's direction. 'Stay and keep her company if it makes you feel better,' he rasped. 'Just don't let her in there with me. I don't want her there, don't you understand?'

'Only too well, Marcus.' Olivia was the one to answer him, turning shakily to walk away. There was only so much of his abuse she could take in her own emotional state. She knew she should never have become his nurse, knew she should never have become involved with the Hamilton family a second time.

'Olivia,' Simon touched her arm gently a few seconds later as she sat outside in one of the luxurious leather armchairs.

She turned with a frown. 'Marcus . . .?'

'In with Fitzgerald. He told me to come after you,' he added gently.

'So that you could pick up the pieces he'd ripped me to?' she said bitterly.

'I think so that you wouldn't leave,' Simon told her softly.

'Isn't that what he wants me to do?' she asked moodily.

'You know it isn't,' he chided. 'At the moment Marcus just wants to hit out at everyone. We just happen to be in the firing line.'

'Yes,' she sighed, some of the tension leaving her. 'I know that really, it's just—well, it doesn't make it any easier to accept his cutting barbs.'

'Because you're emotionally involved,' Simon pointed out gently. 'I'm sure Marcus is far from the first rude patient you've had,' he teased.

'Yes,' she admitted ruefully.

'Then just bear with him for a while longer, hmm?'

'You know I will,' she sighed again. 'I shouldn't let him get to me. I just—I love him,' she stated simply. 'That makes everything about this case different.'

'I understand,' he squeezed her hand. 'But you'll wait here, won't you?'

She nodded. 'How long do you think they'll be?'

'I have no idea,' Simon shrugged. 'I'm going to slip back in in a couple of minutes. Want to come with me?'

Olivia shivered as she envisaged Marcus's anger if she went against his instructions, shaking her head.

But as the time passed she began to wish she had gone with Simon. It was one thing to be in there and see what was going on, it was something else completely to sit out here, the minutes slowly ticking by. After another hour she was almost going crazy wondering how the tests were going. No one had come back into the waiting-area, and no one had come out of the consulting-room in all that time—and she was going insane wondering what was going on behind that brown-painted door.

Ten minutes later it seemed she wouldn't have to wait any longer, a tall fair-haired man leaving the consulting-room, his long easy strides telling of his relaxed state, his mode of dress informal, casual brown trousers and a cream shirt. Somehow she knew this had to be Jason Fitzgerald.

His blue gaze flickered over her impersonally as he closed the door, coming back to rest appreciatively on her face. A tall good-looking man with sun-bleached blond hair and a lithe attractive body, he was confident of his own attraction.

But Olivia was oblivious to his appreciative glances, going over to him anxiously. 'Have you finished your examination?'

Dark brows rose questioningly. 'You would be . . .?' he drawled softly.

'Olivia. Er—Olivia King,' she explained as he still looked puzzled. 'Mr Hamilton's nurse.'

'I didn't think you could be his daughter.' His humour faded, his expression grave. 'How can I help you, Miss King?' His tone was kind.

'How did the examination go? Can you operate?' She couldn't keep the eagerness out of her voice.

'An operation wouldn't do Mr Hamilton the least bit of good. He——'

Olivia didn't hear any more; there was a sudden rushing noise in her head, then blackness forcing in on her. Marcus was going to remain blind for the rest of his life!

CHAPTER SEVEN

'COME on, honey, wake up. Olivia, open your eyes!' the Atlantic drawl ordered briskly.

She reacted to years of training to obey her peers, and opened her eyes slowly, looking up into a friendly bronzed face, sun-bleached fair hair falling forward over the man's forehead. Jason Fitzgerald ... 'Oh God!' she groaned, turning her face into the pillow beneath her on the couch. She frowned. 'Where am I?'

'The consulting-room down the corridor,' Jason Fitzgerald sat on the side of the couch. 'I persuaded Simon Brooks to take your patient home.'

'Oh no!' She closed her eyes, struggling to sit up, swinging her legs to the ground as the specialist stood up. 'What must Marcus think of me?' she groaned.

'He thinks we're having a consultation about him,' Jason drawled reassuringly.

Her shoulders hunched over defeatedly. 'What would be the point? There's nothing to consult about.' Marcus was never going to see again, there was nothing else to say.

The famous specialist shook his head, his mouth twisting wryly. 'You didn't let me finish a few minutes ago,' he reproved. 'If you had you might not have passed out on me in that way.'

Hope began to burn deep within her as she looked at him wide-eyed, swallowing hard, moistening her lips nervously as they suddenly seemed too stiff to move. 'Wh-what do you mean?'

He shrugged broad shoulders, supremely confident of himself and his ability. 'If you had let me finish I would have told you that Marcus Hamilton doesn't need an operation to regain his sight, that in time—and don't ask me to pinpoint that time,' he added at her sudden eagerness. 'He will see as well as you or I—better than me, I happen to wear glasses some of the time,' he mocked.

Olivia knew the last teasing comment was made to lighten her tension, and to a certain degree it worked. 'You mean his blindness is only temporary?' she asked wonderingly.

He nodded. 'He has what we call hysterical blindness. That means—Hey, don't pass out on me again!' he chided impatiently as she paled once more. 'You pass out when you think he's permanently blind, you almost react the same way when I tell you he isn't!' His eyes were narrowed to blue slits. 'Are you sure you're the guy's nurse?'

A deep flush coloured her cheeks under his speculative gaze, and she gave a nervy smile. 'I get involved with my patients,' she excused lamely.

'Hm,' he looked sceptical.

'Marcus Hamilton is the least hysterical man I know,' she declared firmly, wanting to at least regain her authority as a highly qualified nurse.

Jason Fitzgerald smiled. 'I'm sure you know it's just a term for his symptoms. I happen to agree with you, Marcus Hamilton is the least hysterical man I know too. I've heard he's one hell of a good surgeon,' he added thoughtfully. 'And with time he will be again. But to get back to the blindness; he received an emotional blow of some sort before the accident, the bump on the head he received just gave him a good excuse to stop seeing. It's a way of blocking out whatever is troubling him.'

Olivia knew the meaning of the diagnosis, she just couldn't believe it of Marcus. 'You mean he's mentally willing himself not to see?' Even her years of training couldn't comprehend this in connection with Marcus.

'He isn't doing it consciously, honey, his subconscious is doing it for him. There's something he doesn't want to face, something he can't face, so he's evading it in this way. Once the pressure is off he should get his sight back.'

Olivia frowned. 'But what's bothering him?'

'Ah well, if I knew that I wouldn't have needed to have come here, I could have telephoned my diagnosis,' he derided gently. 'I've recommended he see a psychiatrist——'

'And he's refused,' she scoffed, knowing Marcus's reaction to an idea like that.

'You know your patient very well.' The speculative look was back in Jason Fitzgerald's eyes.

'As his nurse I'm supposed to,' she evaded. 'How did Marcus take your diagnosis?'

His mouth twisted. 'Predictably, I imagine,' he smiled. 'He told me I'm a fool.'

'Oh no!'

The specialist chuckled. 'From a man like him I took it as a compliment.'

Her mouth quirked as she joined in his humour. 'It probably was one.'

'I like you, Olivia King,' he smiled across the room at her. 'I don't leave England until tomorrow, how about having dinner with me tonight?'

She flushed at the unexpectedness of the request. Jason Fitzgerald was only in his early forties, was a very attractive man, and yet somehow she hadn't thought of him in that light. She had seen the doctor and not the man, but he certainly hadn't seen just the nurse. She shook her head regretfully. 'Marcus may need me.'

'I'll tell you what, I'm staying at the Hilton, if you find you're free tonight after all, give me a call before seven-thirty. Okay?' he prompted throatily. 'Have pity on a lonely man in a strange country,' he coaxed.

'I have a feeling you don't need to be lonely wherever you are,' she lightly mocked his easy charm.

'I'm trying not to be,' he taunted dryly.

'What happens if I don't telephone before seven-thirty?' she asked thoughtfully.

'You really want to know?'

'You find someone else to spend the evening with?' she laughed softly.

'Exactly,' he returned her grin. 'Although I would enjoy talking to you some more, Olivia.'

She had a feeling he would like to do more than talk, and although she would have liked to talk to him she didn't want any more complications in her life. 'I'll call you before seven-thirty with my answer,' she promised, standing up. 'Now I really should be going, we've taken quite long enough for the consultation,' she teased.

Sally was in with her father when Olivia reached the house, so she took the opportunity to go to her room to freshen up. She still didn't quite feel recovered from her faint, despite a short walk in the fresh air, and her embarrassment about the incident was still acute. If Marcus were ever to know of her reaction he would surely realise she loved him.

Sally knocked on her bedroom door a short time later, and came into the bedroom to sit on the side of the bed as Olivia changed into close-fitting denims and a black tee-shirt, smoothing the latter down over her breasts.

'He doesn't even seem pleased!' Sally finally burst out.

'He is,' she assured the girl. 'He just can't believe it yet.'

'Neither can I,' Sally said shakily. 'Simon told me when I got home, and I expected Daddy to be elated. Instead he seems—Oh, I don't know, distrustful is the word, I think,' she frowned. 'What do you think?'

'I haven't seen him yet.' Olivia sprayed on a liberal amount of her favourite Estée Lauder perfume. 'I'm just going in now.'

'Well, don't expect a fanfare and bright lights,' Sally said despondently. 'Daddy isn't at all pleased by Jason Fitzgerald's diagnosis.'

Olivia found that out for herself a few minutes later!

'Where the hell have you been?' Marcus growled at her angrily.

She had given up questioning how he knew it was her; he just did know. 'With Mr Fitzgerald,' she answered briskly.

'Oh yes?' he sneered. 'You've been consulting with him about me for almost two hours, have you?'

Olivia stiffened at the insult in his tone. 'As a matter of fact, no,' she answered calmly enough. 'I went for a walk after I left the hospital.'

She had needed to be alone for a while before she saw Marcus again, and had spent the last hour wandering around a park in the centre of London. He was going to see again! That was the most important thing to her, and it had been difficult to think past that, to think of the time she would have to leave him. She refused to think about that.

'Oh yes?' Marcus scorned, anger simmering beneath the surface coldness. 'With Fitzgerald?'

'Hardly,' she retorted. 'I just needed some air.'

'He told you his diagnosis?' he rasped.

'Yes.'

'Hysterical blindness!' Marcus said with disgust. 'I think the man's an idiot!'

'So he told me,' she said dryly. 'Marcus——' she began intently, 'the man you went to operate on the night of your accident, what happened to him?'

'Amateur psychology, Olivia?' he taunted.

'Please, Marcus, just answer me.' Hysterical blindness, Jason Fitzgerald had said, difficulty in accepting an emotional blow, he had explained. While walking in the park she had suddenly thought of the man Marcus had operated on the night of his accident, remembering how Marcus had once explained to her that even surgeons were human. 'Please, Marcus,' she repeated softly.

His mouth twisted. 'He left hospital before I did,' he mocked. 'Completely recovered. Try again, Olivia.'

She drew in a ragged breath, disappointed that she hadn't found the key to his emotional block. 'Why do you find it so hard to believe you're going to see again?' she demanded angrily. 'Sally's so excited, and you've put her down. She's depressed now. And I——' she broke off awkwardly.

'Yes?' he prompted hardly. 'I don't suppose you can wait for the time *you* can leave here,' he scorned harshly. 'But think on the positive side of things, Olivia—you've met two new men by being my nurse, Simon and Fitzgerald.'

She flinched at the contempt in his voice. He was deliberately trying to hurt her, was taking his anger and frustration out on her, and in any other circumstances she would have let the insults pass over her. But not from Marcus; she couldn't take that from him.

'And you,' she pointed out softly.

'Me? I don't count,' he rasped.

'Really?' she derided tautly. 'I don't happen to agree with you.'

'Would it surprise you to know I don't give a damn for your opinion?'

Olivia refused to even flinch under his contempt. 'No, it wouldn't,' she replied coolly. 'But you're going to get it anyway. You're going to see again, Marcus, and I for one am ecstatic. I refuse to let you ruin that for me by your insults. Now if you'll excuse me, I have to go.'

'Out with Fitzgerald?' His mouth was tight.

She blinked. 'I beg your pardon?'

'Did Fitzgerald invite you out?' he demanded to know.

'I—He——'

'Did he?'

'Yes, he did,' she flashed. 'But I——'

'I thought so,' drawled Marcus. 'His voice sounded young. How old is he, Olivia?'

She frowned. 'Early forties, I would say.'

'Older than me!'

'Yes. But——'

'Don't let me keep you,' he turned away. 'Fitzgerald sounded very entertaining.'

'I'm sure he is. But——'

'Just get going, Olivia. I wouldn't want you to keep him waiting.'

'I never keep a man waiting,' she snapped, furious with him for making an assumption about her and then not even allowing her to defend herself. 'And I don't intend to make Jason the exception. He's an absolutely fascinating man,' she added spitefully.

'Then go to him, damn you!' Marcus's hands were clenched into tight fists. 'Go to a man who can satisfy you,' he muttered.

'What did you say?' she gasped.

'I have good reason to know you're a highly sensual woman, Olivia,' his mouth twisted. 'And last night didn't quite meet up to your expectations, did it?'

Her breathing was ragged as she tried to control her temper. It didn't work! 'I didn't expect anything of you, you tried to take something of mine.'

'Not your virginity! You lost that years ago,' he jeered scornfully.

She gasped at his vehemence. 'That's right,' she bit out furiously. 'I did. So one more man won't matter, will it? Go back to your self-pity, Marcus, but don't expect me to join in!' She slammed out of the room with great fury, shaking so much she felt ready to collapse.

The Hayes family were the best antidote Olivia could think of to a breaking heart; and her heart was breaking, into a thousand tiny pieces.

She had telephoned the Hilton before leaving the house to tell Jason Fitzgerald that she couldn't meet him, and had then driven over to see the Hayes. Rick and Natalie were out for the evening, but Clara and Eric were very welcoming.

'How is Marcus progressing?' Clara asked interestedly.

It was the perfect opportunity to tell them of the visit to the hospital today, and she spent the next few minutes doing just that, not realising how much she was revealing until she saw the warmth of compassion in Clara's eyes. The older woman might be a little scatty to live with, but she had the usual amount of feminine intuition. Olivia looked away with a blush.

'Eric, how about a nice cup of tea?' Clara prompted her husband.

'Hm?' He roused himself from his slouched position in the chair, having been watching television as the two women talked quietly.

'Tea, dear,' Clara repeated in a firm voice.

'Oh—okay.' He got to his feet, blinking his surprise; his wife wasn't usually this forceful.

'Men!' Clara sighed dryly once he had left the room. 'They have no idea when they aren't wanted,' she shook her head. 'How is Marcus really? We would have liked to come and visit him, but Sally says he still feels uncomfortable about his blindness.'

'He's unbearable,' Olivia responded bluntly. 'Totally unbearable,' she repeated shakily. 'And rude. And insulting. He's just awful!' She shuddered at the emotional pressure she had been working under these last weeks.

'And you love him very much,' Clara added softly.

'Yes,' sighed Olivia, putting her hands up to her face. 'God, I just had to get away from him for a while!'

'I understand,' the other woman said gently. 'I suspected something like this from the first day you met Sally at the pool party. You seemed to change that day, and then there was Sally's call later. But I'm not going to pry, my dear, that isn't what friends are for. And both you and Marcus are our friends. Why don't you stay here tonight? Give yourself a break from it.'

'I couldn't.'

'Why not?'

Why not? It had been agreed that Saturday would be her day off, and a simple telephone call to Sally would make sure there was no concern as to her absence. Marcus, unless told otherwise by Sally, would put a different construction on her actions, she had no doubt, but at the moment she didn't particularly care what he chose to think.

'Your old room can easily be made up,' Clara encouraged as she saw her hesitation. 'And as recompense for taking care of him all that time Rick can bring you breakfast in bed in the morning,' she added teasingly.

Olivia had to smile at this suggestion. 'I think that might be rather nice,' she gratefully accepted the invitation to stay.

'Good,' said Clara with satisfaction. 'While you call Sally I'll go and tell Eric he can come back into the room now.' She left with a serene smile.

Olivia put the call through to Sally before she changed her mind. The evenings were basically her own anyway, and with the whole day to herself tomorrow she was free to do what she wanted.

'Sally isn't here at the moment,' Miss Podmore told her. 'And Mrs Carr went to her room over an hour ago. I'll put you through to Mr Hamilton.'

'Oh no——' Too late, she could already hear the call being put through to the extension in Marcus's room!

'Yes?' he barked unwelcomingly.

She moistened her lips nervously, not having expected to talk to Marcus himself. After the way they had parted earlier she didn't know what to say to him.

'Well?' he snapped at her continued silence. 'Who is that?'

'Olivia,' she told him huskily.

'Olivia?' he repeated sharply. 'What's wrong? Are you hurt?' His voice had deepened with concern.

'No—no, nothing like that,' she hastily assured him. 'I just—I won't be coming back to the house tonight, and I—I didn't want anyone to worry.'

There was silence for several minutes. 'You don't have to do this, Olivia,' Marcus spoke gently.

'Do what?'

'I'm sorry for the things I said earlier,' he didn't answer her question. 'I had no right to pass judgment on your morals. Come home, Olivia.'

'I——'

'Olivia, I have—Oh, sorry,' Eric's voice lowered to a whisper as he realised she was still on the telephone. 'I didn't know,' he grimaced before leaving the room again.

'Was that Fitzgerald?' Marcus demanded harshly. 'Of course it was,' he answered himself. 'I'm sorry, Olivia,' his voice was heavily laced with sarcasm now, 'I didn't realise he was the reason you weren't coming back tonight. I didn't know you were into one night stands.'

Olivia didn't dignify this last insult with an answer, slowly replacing the receiver, composing her features before joining Clara and Eric in the kitchen, sipping gratefully at her waiting cup of tea.

'I didn't interrupt anything important, did I?' Eric frowned at her pale face.

'No, nothing important.' She gave a bright smile. 'I—I think I'll go to bed now. Would you mind?'

'Not at all,' Clara encouraged softly. 'You know the way.'

Olivia had been lying wide-eyed in the bed for almost an hour when she heard Clara and Eric go to their bedroom, grateful when the other woman didn't try to talk to her about Marcus again tonight; she would probably have broken down and cried.

Marcus's verbal attacks were becoming more and more personal, and she wasn't sure how much more she could take. It was one thing to tell him she was staying, quite another to continue working with those cruel barbs day after day. Maybe the instantaneous physical response she had to him had given him reason to question her morals, but she couldn't help loving him, couldn't help wanting him. And if that made her a wanton in his eyes then so be it.

'Wakey, wakey!' greeted a cheerful voice. 'Breakfast in bed for the lovely lady!' Rick added encouragingly.

Olivia was buried far below the bedclothes, and she felt far from lovely; her eyes felt gritty and sore from lack of sleep, and her whole body seemed to ache with fatigue. It had been the early hours of the morning before she drifted off to sleep, and her head ached from lack of rest.

'Are you in there?' Rick teased.

'I think so,' she muttered, emerging from beneath the blankets, blinking at the bright daylight that shone in through the lemon curtains. 'Okay, okay,' she laughed softly as Rick's eyes widened. 'I know I don't look my best first thing in the morning—but I'm sure I can't look as bad as a certain young man I remember waking up for three months,' she mocked, sitting up, the sheet pulled up beneath her chin to cover her nakedness.

Rick grinned, as goodnatured as usual, handing her a cup of tea. 'No, you aren't that bad—you just have coal sacks beneath your eyes!'

'I love you too!' she grimaced.

'I know,' he said cheekily. 'Come on, hurry and get up. Natalie and I are taking you out with us this morning.'

'You are?' she smiled, sipping her tea.

'We are,' he nodded. 'So don't be long.' He moved to the door, turning back with a wicked grin. 'Mum always used to pull the bedclothes off me if I wouldn't get up,' he told her threateningly.

Olivia's fingers tightened about the sheet. 'Don't you dare!'

He was laughing his enjoyment as he went back downstairs. Olivia lay back against the pillows with a weary sigh, her smile fading. She was so tired, it was hard to keep her eyes open. The last thing she felt like doing was going out.

And yet she was determined to enjoy her day off, knew she would return to Marcus's taunts soon enough. Besides, it was a matter of pride to her, a matter of not letting Marcus know how deeply he could upset her. She would not crawl back to the house as if she were guilty of something.

It was for that reason and that reason alone that she presented herself downstairs ten minutes later, the toast and tea Rick had brought up to her consumed in spite of her lack of appetite.

'Ready?' Rick stood up as she entered the kitchen. 'I told Natalie we'd pick her up at her home.'

'Can I come?' his sister asked shyly.

'Why not?' Rick ruffled her hair affectionately.

In the end it was a family trip. Rick drove them out

of London to Woburn in Bedfordshire, spending the day looking around the magnificent estate of the Duke of Bedford, driving around the safari park he had made of the extensive grounds.

'It always seems a shame to me that those people are reduced to doing that to what is basically their home,' Clara said wistfully on the drive back to London later that afternoon.

'It's either that, or a lot of these stately homes would have to be sold,' Eric pointed out.

'Why are men so practical?' the other woman grimaced at Olivia.

'We can be romantic when we need to be,' Rick put in teasingly, and received a glaring look from Natalie.

They all laughed together, having managed to squash into Eric's station-wagon for this enjoyable day out in the country.

It was after six when they got back to London, and Olivia refused the offer to have dinner with them all, deciding she really should get back to the Hamiltons'. Marcus might be a cruel devil of a man, but he was still her patient, her responsibility.

Sally and her grandmother were in the lounge when she entered the house, Sally telling her that Marcus was refusing to leave his room again, that he had shunned company all day.

'Did you have an enjoyable day—and night, Miss King?' Sybil Carr asked bitchily.

Her mouth tightened. 'Very nice, thank you.' She pretended to take the query at face value, knowing very well it hadn't been meant to be. 'I'll just go up and see my patient, if you'll excuse me.' She left the room before the other woman could throw out any more insults.

She couldn't ever remember working anywhere where so much resentment was shown to her!

Marcus stiffened as she entered his room, staring

sightlessly out of the window, although it was obvious he knew she was there. Jasper came over to greet her, having none of the reserve of his master, and at last allowed into the house. This softening attitude towards the dog pleased Olivia.

'You came back, then,' Marcus suddenly rasped.

She walked over to stand beside his chair, Jasper at her heels. 'I told you I wouldn't be forced into leaving,' she said huskily, wishing she could ease that frown between his eyes.

'I smell a different aftershave this time,' he bit out, his expression stony.

'Really?' she asked uninterestedly.

'Yes, I—It wasn't Fitzgerald,' he realised suspiciously.

'No.'

'Some other man?' he frowned.

'That's right,' Olivia confirmed.

'Who?'

'Just a man,' she dismissed.

'Just a——! I can't believe this of you, Olivia.' His hands clenched. 'It isn't like you.'

'How do you know what I'm like?' she scorned.

'You sound sweet and—and innocent.'

'I thought I had a "hard little voice"?' she reminded him dryly.

'You do,' his mouth twisted. 'Sometimes. At others it can be soft and gentle. Why do we argue so much, Olivia?' His mood changed, became softer, less bitter.

'*We* don't—*you* do.'

He gave an angry sigh. 'Who was the man, Olivia?'

'Just an old friend,' she evaded.

'Do you have a lot of "old friends"?'

'Quite a few. I have a lot of new ones too,' she added defiantly. 'As you've already mentioned.'

'Why did you change your mind about Fitzgerald?' he rasped. 'You said you were seeing him last night.'

'A woman doesn't have to give a reason for changing her mind. Sally tells me you've been fine since I've been away,' she changed the subject, her tone professionally brisk.

'What does she know?' he scowled.

'She takes her studies very seriously. I think she'll make a good doctor.'

'In your expert opinion?' he sneered harshly.

'Exactly,' she bit out. 'Well, you seem in your normal pleasantly charming mood,' she scorned, 'so I'll leave you alone. I need an early night.'

'Tired?' he tormented suggestively.

'As a matter of fact, yes,' she flashed. 'I didn't sleep much last night. And I doubt I'll have breakfast brought to me in bed tomorrow morning either,' she added with challenge.

His brows rose. 'A considerate lover!'

'Yes, very considerate. Do you need anything before I go?'

'What I *need* you can't give me.' His mouth was tight. 'But I'll take some sleeping pills.'

She went to get them from the adjoining bathroom. 'You should be starting to ease up on these now.' She handed him a glass of water to help get them down.

'It's the only way I can get any sleep,' he bit out grimly. 'Unless you have a better idea?'

'Not one,' she dismissed coldly, too conscious of the last time she had tried to help him with his insomnia.

Sally had already gone up to her room when Olivia got downstairs, Sybil Carr now alone in the lounge. Olivia was at once wary of the other woman, having good reason to know this woman didn't like her.

Tonight didn't look like being any different from the other occasions they had spoken. 'So you changed your mind, Miss King,' Sybil drawled contemptuously.

Olivia moistened her lips tentatively, wondering

what bees' nest she was about to bring down on her head this time. 'About what?' she asked slowly.

'About making yourself indispensable to Marcus—in some ways.'

She drew in a sharp breath. 'A nurse can't help but——'

'I meant as a woman, Miss King.' Sybil eyed her confidently, perfectly assured as she sat in one of the armchairs, looking as attractive as usual, not a hair out of place. 'You see, I occasionally suffer from insomnia . . .'

Olivia stiffened. 'Yes?'

'And when that happens I find it helps to take a walk . . .'

'Yes?'

'Which is what I did Thursday night,' Sybil added pointedly.

Olivia clenched her hands together to stop their shaking, knowing what was coming next. She had never met such a venomous woman as Sybil Carr!

The older woman's mouth twisted with contempt. 'Did you really think Marcus's visits to your bedroom would go unnoticed?' she scorned.

'Mrs Carr——'

The woman stood gracefully to her feet. 'I just wanted you to know that your unprofessional behaviour has been noted, that I know exactly how far you are willing to go as regards your patient's welfare. But remember one thing, Miss King, you were dispensable to him once—and you will be again. Highly dispensable,' she added dismissively.

Olivia knew she couldn't go on with this much longer; the whole situation was impossible. And what would Marcus say if he knew Sybil, his beloved Ruth's mother, was aware of the time he had spent in his nurse's bedroom?

CHAPTER EIGHT

'No improvement,' Simon told her on Monday afternoon after he had examined Marcus and they had both gone downstairs to the lounge.

Olivia grimaced. 'None at all?'

'Not that I can see,' he shook his head. 'Mentally I would say he's worse.'

She knew that, had detected a subtle change about Marcus that was difficult to define. He no longer argued with her, but was chillingly polite, his depression of a week ago back in full force.

'He's stopped fighting, hasn't he?' Simon said with a frown.

'Yes,' she agreed huskily.

'What happened?'

'I don't know,' she shrugged her confusion. 'I really have no idea. We had an argument on Saturday evening when I got back, but since then, nothing.'

He sighed. 'It's a strange form of therapy,' he gave a rueful smile. 'But with Marcus it was working.'

Olivia nodded. 'But not any more. What do we do now?'

'Leave it for a while, I think,' he said thoughtfully. 'This mood could pass.'

'And if it doesn't?'

'Then we rethink our strategy.'

She smiled. 'You make it sound like a war!'

'Sometimes I think it is,' Simon muttered. 'Marcus against us. He's going to see again if it's the last thing I do!'

'That's what I like to hear!' Sally came exuberantly

into the room like her usual whirlwind. 'I've just been up to see him. How do you think he is?'

'No better,' Simon answered truthfully.

'He will be,' the girl said with certainty. 'I have faith in you both.'

'Thanks!' Simon said dryly.

'Don't you like compliments?' Sally taunted, eyeing him challengingly.

Olivia watched as Simon flushed. For such a talented and accomplished man he was very bashful in front of Sally. And the young girl knew it too! She could see the feminine knowledge burning in Sally's eyes, eyes that glowed with mischief—and something else. For the second time she began to wonder if Simon's interest weren't more than returned.

'If they're sincere, yes,' he answered dryly.

'Oh, mine always are.' Sally threw herself down into a chair, dangling one denim-clad leg over its arm. 'I'm basically an honest person.'

'Basically a cheeky one.' Simon stood up. 'I'll call again in a couple of days,' he told Olivia. 'Unless you need me before that.'

'You aren't leaving already?' Sally pouted her disappointment.

'I have to, little one,' he gave a gentle smile. 'The hospital doesn't run itself, and with your father away . . .'

She nodded slowly, although the disappointment was still reflected in the grey of her eyes. 'I understand. I'll see you to the door, shall I?'

'That isn't necessary——'

'Oh, but I want to.' She stood up agilely.

'The energy of the young,' Simon grimaced, weary himself as he obviously felt the strain of Marcus's absence from the hospital, having been carrying the double workload for a couple of months now.

Sally flushed. 'You know your trouble?' she snapped.

'No, but I'm sure you're going to tell me,' he quirked blond brows.

'I told you, I'm basically an honest person,' she said impudently. 'You should get out more, Simon, before you get too old.'

Olivia held back her splutter of laughter with effort. Listening to these two as they verbally fenced was guaranteed to lighten anyone's mood.

'You remember that smacked bottom I once threatened you with?' he drawled, deceptively softly.

Sally grinned. 'Yes?'

'You're getting dangerously close to it!'

'Sounds interesting,' she quipped as she walked to the door with him.

Olivia was still chuckling when Sally came back to the lounge a few minutes later. 'You're really going to push him too far one of these days,' she warned lightly.

'I hope so,' the girl sighed. 'I'm running out of ways to attract his interest.'

'And do you want it?'

'Olivia, before I answer that, will you tell me something?'

She frowned at Sally's intensity. 'I should think so,' she nodded.

'Do you like Simon?'

'Of course I—Not in that way, no,' Olivia realised the reason for the question. 'I like him as a person and a doctor, but I have no interest in him as a lover.'

'Sure?' Sally still didn't look convinced.

She smiled. 'Very. And you?'

'Oh, I've been sure of Simon since I was fifteen years old,' the girl told her confidently. 'At least, sure of my own feelings for him. I'm going to marry him.'

'Sally!' Olivia gasped her incredulity.

'But I am,' Sally nodded. 'Daddy and I are both like that, once our love is given we never take it back. But

I just wanted to make sure you weren't interested in Simon. I wanted to ask him out to a party, but I didn't want to tread on your toes.'

'Invite away,' smiled Olivia.

Sally grimaced. 'He's a little old-fashioned about some things, he might not like my asking him out.'

'There's no harm in trying. He should be back at the hospital in a few minutes, why don't you call him?'

'Oh, I don't know . . .'

'Where's all that confidence now?' teased Olivia.

'You're right,' Sally said determinedly. 'He can only say no.' She went out to use the telephone in the hallway.

Olivia had the feeling that far from saying no Simon would grasp at the fact that it was Sally asking him out, a sure indication that she was attracted to him too.

'He said yes!' Sally came back into the room a few minutes later. 'He said yes, Olivia,' she repeated dazedly.

Olivia's mouth quirked. 'What did you want him to say?'

'Well—yes. But I never thought he would.' Sally sat down with a thump. 'I told him it was just a few of the kids from college getting together, that he would probably be bored with us juvenile delinquents. And he still said yes!'

'I'm pleased for you,' smiled Olivia.

'Do you think I did the right thing?' Sally chewed on her bottom lip in the aftermath of uncertainty. 'What if we get to the party and he really *does* think I'm too juvenile for him?' She looked at Olivia with troubled grey eyes.

'I'm sure that won't happen,' she soothed gently. 'If it does you can always tell him he's wrong.'

Sally flushed at the gentle taunt. 'Do you think I was too outspoken earlier?'

Olivia could see that the doubt was really beginning

to set in now, and although she was sure Sally wouldn't believe her right now she was sure the younger girl's dreams of one day marrying Simon would come true; they could hardly do anything else when confronted with such determination!

'I'm sure Simon didn't think so,' she reassured the girl. 'It got a reaction, didn't it,' she shrugged. 'And he's going to the party with you.'

'Yes,' Sally grinned. 'Yes, he is.' She looked pleased with herself.

'If you intend marrying Simon,' Olivia mocked, 'what are you going to do about your career? I thought you were determined to become a doctor?'

'I am, and I'm going to be. Simon isn't the man I think he is if he expects me to give up my career when we're married.'

She had it all worked out, and Olivia could only admire her certainty about the future. It must be wonderful to have your life all mapped out, to know what you wanted and be determined to get it. She had known who and what she wanted at eighteen too, it just hadn't worked out for her. She had a feeling Sally was going to be luckier than she had been.

'I'm sure he won't,' she told Sally, standing up. 'I'd better get back to your father, I told him I would only be a few minutes, and that was almost half an hour ago.'

Sally frowned. 'Do you think I should tell him I'm seeing Simon?'

Olivia thought about it for a few minutes. 'Maybe not just yet,' she answered at last. 'I think he has enough to think about at the moment without being told his daughter has picked out the man she intends to marry.'

The younger girl laughed. 'Maybe you're right. I wouldn't want to shock him.'

Olivia wasn't sure Marcus was capable of being

shocked by anything at the moment, the lethargy that seemed to have possessed him not lessening at all over the next few weeks. His politeness became such that it frustrated her to talk to him, and he seemed unaware of the fact that his daughter was spending more and more evenings away from the house. Olivia could only be pleased for Sally, her relationship with Simon obviously proving to be everything she had hoped it would be, her uncertainties all for nothing as their love flourished. Simon now had the look of a man who had been given his greatest happiness, as indeed he probably had.

Marcus seemed unaware of Sally's inner happiness, although Simon's new-found exuberance with life didn't escape him.

'I take it your—friendship with Simon is progressing nicely,' Marcus remarked scornfully two weeks later after the other man paid him another professional call.

The obvious thing for her to do was to correct the wrong assumption he had made that Simon's interest was in her, but after days of receiving only apathy from him she knew she should take advantage of this show of temperament. 'And if it is?' she challenged.

'Nothing.'

She almost sighed her frustration as he once again dropped behind that cloak of uninterest. 'He's a very thoughtful and interesting—man.'

Marcus's expression darkened over her slight hesitation. 'That's nice for you,' he returned tightly.

'I think——'

'Could I have tea now?' he requested abruptly.

This time Olivia did sigh her frustration. 'If that's what you want,' she said dully.

'I already told you, what I want you can't give me,' he snapped.

'What do you want, Marcus?' She was suddenly angry herself, days of his cold politeness having grated on her nerves. 'Sympathy for your blindness?' she demanded harshly. 'You won't get it,' she told him heatedly. 'Not from me! You sit in that chair day after day, making no attempt to discover what's causing the mental block that stops you seeing, refusing the help I tried to give you——'

'I don't need your help, I already know why I can't see!'

She gave him a sharp disbelieving look for this flat statement. 'Marcus . . .?'

His knuckles showed white as his hands gripped about the arms of the chair. 'Would you just go and get my tea?' he grated.

'But if you know——'

'Knowing hasn't helped, has it! I refuse to discuss this with you any further,' Marcus bit out coldly at her persistence.

She swallowed hard at this cruel dismissal in his tone. 'Me especially, or just anyone?' she voiced softly, tense as she waited for his answer.

'Does it matter?'

To her—yes! If it had got to the stage where she was actually hindering his recovery then she would have to stop being his nurse. 'Yes,' she told him simply.

'I——'

'Would you mind leaving us, Miss King?' interrupted the autocratic voice of Sybil Carr. 'I want to talk to my son-in-law,' she added with arrogance. 'Alone.'

Olivia looked with unhidden surprise at the other woman. Not once since Marcus's return home had she made any effort to visit him; for her to come to his room after all this time and demand to see him left Olivia speechless for a moment. She could see Marcus was as stunned as she.

'Sybil?' he frowned.

His mother-in-law avoided looking at him directly, something Marcus couldn't possibly be aware of, but which Olivia was very much so. Whatever it was Sybil wanted to discuss with Marcus, she was no closer to accepting his blindness.

'I need to talk to you, Marcus,' Sybil said awkwardly.

His mouth twisted as he sensed her reluctance. 'This is an unexpected pleasure,' he drawled.

Sybil's mouth tightened at his mockery. 'Would you mind, Miss King?' she snapped pointedly.

'Not at all,' Olivia replied coolly. 'I was about to go downstairs for our tea anyway. Perhaps you would like to join us?'

Sybil barely contained her shudder of distaste for the idea. 'I've already had mine,' she answered with obvious relief. 'Besides, what I have to say won't take long.'

'Sounds ominous,' Marcus said dryly as Olivia turned to leave.

'Not at all,' his mother-in-law replied tersely. 'It's about my trip to France——'

Olivia didn't hear any more, but closed the door softly behind her. It was obvious that Sybil Carr still couldn't handle the trauma of Marcus's illness, and it sounded as if she had decided to remove herself from having to face it.

Although Olivia couldn't thank her for interrupting her conversation with Marcus. For the first time in days she had been about to have a heated exchange with him, something she felt they needed badly, although the subject of that conversation had been upsetting to her.

She was still brooding on it thoughtfully as she returned up the stairs with their tea-tray, almost dropping it as she heard the voices raised in anger.

'France is out of the question for me at the moment, you know that, Sybil,' Marcus rasped.

'It's only common decency——'

'And I'm only blind!' came his cutting reply.

'Ruth was your wife,' Sybil reminded him heatedly.

'She's dead,' he said dully.

'That's my point exactly,' his mother-in-law snapped.

'Would she have done the same for me, do you think?' Marcus asked with quiet bitterness.

'I don't——'

'You know damn well she wouldn't,' he bit out tautly. 'And that's the end of the matter as far as I'm concerned,' he added hardly.

'It always was,' Sybil replied furiously. 'And I suppose your attitude has done nothing to influence Sally into refusing to come with me too?'

'Sally's actions are her own affair,' Marcus replied stiffly.

Olivia was too stunned by the vehemence of the conversation to move, despite knowing she was overhearing a very personal discussion.

'It's been three years, Sybil,' Marcus's voice softened reasoningly. 'You don't have to continue with this pilgrimage.'

'Ruth was my daughter,' came the stiff answer. 'And if neither you or Sally will come with me then I'll go to France alone.'

'That's your prerogative.'

'I might have known this would be your answer,' Sybil accused raggedly. 'I told Ruth she should never have married you, you never really loved her, only wanted the money and influence she could give you to further your career.'

'Sybil——'

'Don't deny it, Marcus,' she snapped. 'You know it's the truth. You broke my little girl's heart with your coldness, forced her into the arms of another man.'

There was no answer from Marcus, and in the

circumstances Olivia could understand why. Marcus had loved his wife very much, had forgiven Ruth's indiscretion to take her back into his life—now to be accused of breaking *her* heart was ludicrous. Although the rest of the conversation was a bit of a puzzle to her. Why should Sybil want Marcus and Sally to go to France with her, and what did it have to do with Ruth?

'I shall be leaving as soon as possible,' Sybil rasped. 'This evening, if it can be arranged.'

'You must please yourself,' came his abrupt reply.

'I intend to. I find it distasteful to stay in this house with you and your mistress—'

'My *what?*'

'Perhaps that's a rather old-fashioned description of your relationship with Miss King,' Sybil sneered. 'But for the moment I can't think of a better one!'

'Leave Olivia out of this,' Marcus bit out fiercely.

'I've said all I had to say,' Sybil snapped. 'Although I think you should consider the example you're setting for Sally.'

'Goodbye, Sybil,' he said woodenly.

'You can't deny that Sally is much too young to be going out with Simon Brooks.'

'Simon?' Sharp interest deepened in Marcus's voice.

'The two of them have been seeing each other for the last two weeks,' his mother-in-law informed him haughtily. 'It's a totally unsuitable match for Sally.'

'Don't you mean Olivia?'

'Don't be ridiculous, Marcus,' Sybil replied shortly. 'I'm well aware of the fact that you've been sleeping with your nurse. I even saw you leave her bedroom one night. How can Sally hope to have any idea of real love when you flaunt your affair in front of her?'

'How long has this conversation been going on?'

Olivia turned sharply at the softly spoken query,

paling as she saw Sally was standing just behind her. How much of the conversation had the girl heard? How much did she need to have heard to know that Marcus had visited his nurse's bedroom at least once!

'I'm surprised it hasn't happened before,' Sally continued in a whisper. 'Daddy and Grandmother invariably fight at this time of year.'

Maybe they did, but as far as Olivia knew it was the first time she had been part of the reason for that argument.

'You mustn't let it bother you, Olivia,' Sally squeezed her arm reassuringly. 'You and I are only secondary matters in this, Grandmother's real complaint is that Daddy and I won't go to France to visit Mummy's grave with her.'

Olivia frowned her surprise. 'Your mother is buried in France?'

'Mm,' Sally nodded. 'Daddy is of the opinion that visiting a person's grave once a year can in no way make up for the things that happened while they were alive. I happen to agree with him.' She grimaced. 'Grandmother doesn't, she thinks it shows a lack of respect.'

'I'm afraid she's also told your father about yourself and Simon,' Olivia revealed softly, her thoughts spinning.

The young girl shrugged. 'It was no secret.' She looked down at the tea-tray Olivia was clutching so tightly. 'Shall I take this in for you? That way Daddy and I can have a talk once Grandmother has left.'

Olivia pushed the tray at the other girl, anxious to go to the privacy of her bedroom, unable to face Marcus after the accusations Sybil Carr had made about the two of them, accusations he had made no effort to deny. 'Thank you,' she accepted stiffly. 'I would like to freshen up.'

Sally gave her an understanding smile, bracing her

own shoulders to enter her father's bedroom. Olivia
didn't wait for the outcome of that, but escaped to her
bedroom, hearing the door to Marcus's room slam
loudly a few seconds later. Sybil Carr had obviously
finished all that she had to say.

Why had Ruth Hamilton been in France when she
died? And why was Marcus still so bitter about his
wife, hadn't the reconciliation been a success after all?

CHAPTER NINE

IT took all Olivia's willpower to go to Marcus's room later that evening, her duties as his nurse making it impossible for her to evade the confrontation. Although Sally had assured her that there wouldn't be one, that she had explained everything to her father. What worried Olivia was the 'everything' she had explained! That Sally and Simon were seeing each other, seriously, would most certainly have been explained—and only minutes before Olivia had been claiming her own relationship with him. Marcus was going to think her a fool on top of everything else he thought of her.

He was lying on his bed when she entered the room, the dark glasses firmly in place, his arm thrown back on the pillow behind his head. But the impression that he might be asleep was dispelled the moment she closed the door softly behind her, and his body at once tensed.

He turned in her direction. 'Olivia?'

'The one and only,' she confirmed lightly, moving further into the room.

Marcus sat up to swing his feet down on to the ground. 'Why did you lie to me?'

Olivia swallowed hard at this direct attack, not surprised by it—she knew Marcus too well for that!— but disconcerted anyway. 'Lie to you?' she prevaricated, standing some distance away from him. 'Why should I have lied to you?'

'That's what I'm trying to find out,' he said hardly. 'Sally told me she's the one who has been seeing Simon. Why let me think it was you?'

'Did I?'

'You know damn well you did!' he accused harshly. 'And Fitzgerald?'

'Your specialist, nothing more.' Her hands were tightly linked together in front of her.

'And the man you spent the night with, the one who brings you breakfast in bed?' he scorned.

She drew in a controlling breath. 'I visited Clara and Eric Hayes, and they very kindly invited me to spend the night and following day with them. Their son Rick was the one who brought me breakfast in bed. What did you say?' she asked as Marcus muttered something under his breath.

'I said damn you!' he repeated fiercely. 'Why did you do that to me?' he demanded. 'Aren't I enough of a cripple without making me feel less of a man by flaunting your other lovers in my face?'

Olivia had paled at the accusation, the defensive hand she put up dropping lifelessly back to her side. 'I didn't do that. I only——'

'You only made me feel inadequate, incapable of being your lover! And to think I've been sitting here in this chair wishing to be just that!' he derided himself.

She was the reason for his depression of the last few weeks?

'Marcus——'

'Get out of here, Olivia.' He turned away from her. 'And that isn't a request, it's an order. I don't think I can bear to have you around me any more.'

'I'll leave you alone for a while,' she agreed desperately, very much afraid that he meant much more than that. 'I can come back at dinner, and then we——'

'I meant I think you should go from the house, Olivia,' he told her dully. 'I don't need you here any more.'

'But——'

'You know it's true,' he continued remorselessly. 'I'm taking no medication, not even sleeping pills,' he mocked her constant nagging at him to discontinue them, something he had acquiesced to several days ago. Whether or not he was sleeping without them he hadn't told her, and she hadn't liked to ask. 'I don't need a nurse any longer, you know it and so do I.'

'I——'

'It will be better for everyone if you leave, best for you and certainly best for me.' His face was averted from her, his expression rigid. 'I no longer need a nurse,' he repeated determinedly.

'How about a friend?'

He turned on her fiercely at the softly spoken question. 'You and I could never be friends,' he bit out icily.

'That isn't true——'

'I don't want to be your friend, Olivia.' Marcus stood up to move forcefully about the room. 'But then you already knew that, have been aware of it since the first.'

'The first?' she repeated sharply, instantly alerted.

'Since the moment you walked into my hospital room and started tormenting me with your hard little voice, throwing out those tiny barbs to get a response. Oh, of course I knew what you were doing,' he mocked her dismayed gasp, his mouth twisting. 'But underneath the anger was a sexual awareness, an awareness you may not have been averse to exploring. Unfortunately it didn't meet up to my expectations. It no longer suits me to have you here,' he added cruelly.

She swallowed hard. 'I see,' she moistened suddenly dry lips. 'I'll have to have Simon's approval before I go—after all, he is your doctor.'

Marcus breathed harshly. 'I'm also a doctor, and I'm quite capable of deciding that I can manage without a nurse. You asked me earlier if it's just you I won't discuss my blindness with.' He turned directly towards her. 'I believe it is.'

She gave a choked cry, feeling as if he had just struck her, as indeed verbally he had.

'Would it be too soon for you to leave tomorrow?'

She gulped, knowing that this time there was to be no respite, that Marcus was implacable. 'Not if that's when you want me to go.'

'I think so,' he nodded woodenly. 'And, Olivia . . .' he stopped her as she reached the door.

'Yes?' she turned eagerly, hope fading as she saw he wasn't even looking her way.

'I'm pleased about Sally and Simon. I'm sure they'll be happy together.'

'Yes,' she agreed dully, 'so am I. Sally is a young woman who knows what she wants.' And got it. Oh, how she wished she could have the man she wanted too, the man she *loved*. But he was turning her out of his house, out of his life, probably for ever.

Marcus didn't answer her; the conversation was over as far as he was concerned. The whole thing was over as far as he was concerned, now he just wanted to get on with the rest of his life, without her help. And he was right, medically he no longer needed her, and now that their verbal disputes had more or less come to an end he no longer needed her for mental stimulation. And he no longer needed her because he wasn't attracted to her sexually any more! Oh, how she wished she had realised the attraction, she would have taken any opportunity she could to be in his arms.

Simon was as disappointed with her leaving as she was, but like her, there was nothing he could do about it if Marcus had made up his mind. She managed to keep her own mind a blank as she began to pack her things into the two cases she had brought with her when she arrived a few weeks ago, her dejection not entirely due to the fact that she had failed Marcus as a nurse, she had failed him as a woman too, had made him feel less than the sensually attractive man he would always be. It *would* be better for them all if she left now.

She looked up as a light knock sounded on the door, her hopes dying an instant death as logic took over. Marcus hadn't given the impression that he ever wanted to see or talk to her again, and even if he did he wasn't likely to knock. He hadn't the previous time he had come to her room. 'Come in,' she invited almost wearily, her assumptions proving correct when Sally walked into the room.

'Grandmother is busy packing, and——What's going on?' the younger girl frowned as she saw the open suitcases on Olivia's bed, both of them partially full as she continued to put her neatly folded clothes inside the suitcase behind her. 'Are you leaving?' Sally realised slowly.

'That seems to be the general idea,' Olivia answered brightly.

'But why? I don't understand.' Sally came to sit on the bed next to the cases. 'Have you and Daddy argued again? You don't have to leave because of that, I'm sure he'll have forgotten about it by tomorrow.'

'We haven't argued,' Olivia assured her.

'Then why this?' Sally held up one of the skirts from the suitcase.

'Hey,' Olivia reprimanded gently, 'I've just packed that!'

'Sorry.' The girl put it neatly back in place. 'But why are you leaving, is it because of what Grandmother said about you earlier? She doesn't understand——'

'Your grandmother has nothing to do with my going,' Olivia told Sally truthfully, not halting in her packing, needing to have something to do with her hands so that the other girl shouldn't see how they were trembling.

'She's leaving herself tomorrow, she couldn't get a flight today——'

'It has nothing to do with your grandmother,' Olivia repeated forcefully, her cool reserve breaking momentarily. She took a deep controlling breath. 'Your father and I have—talked, and decided I'm no longer necessary.'

'But——'

'And Simon agrees,' she added softly.

Sally's eyes widened at the mention of his name, her respect for Simon having deepened during the time they had been going out together, and she very much valued his opinion. 'He does?' she asked uncertainly.

'He does,' Olivia nodded.

Sally still looked puzzled. 'Are you sure you and Daddy haven't argued? All this is a bit sudden, isn't it?'

'I suppose so,' Olivia shrugged, her nerves becoming taut with the tension of getting through this conversation. 'But once a nurse is no longer—needed, then she—she may as well go,' her voice began to quiver. 'That was the only reason I was able to come here so promptly in the first place, you know that. Now don't you think you should go and talk to your grandmother?' she reprimanded gently. 'She seems rather upset that you won't go to France with her.'

'She always is,' Sally dismissed.

Olivia schooled her expression to remain only casually interested. 'What was your mother doing in France when she—when she died? Were you all on holiday there?'

Sally shook her head. 'Mummy lived there.'

'In France?' Olivia gasped. What was Ruth Hamilton doing living in France when Marcus had never moved out of London?

'Mm,' the girl nodded. 'But surely you knew that?' she frowned.

Olivia looked startled by the assumption. 'Why should I know where your mother lived?'

'I thought Daddy might have mentioned it to you,' Sally shrugged. 'Mummy went to live there after they separated.'

'But surely—I thought she came back,' Olivia said dazedly.

'Sometimes, for holidays, things like that,' Sally nodded. 'But my stepfather was never keen on coming to England.' She grimaced. 'I can't say I ever liked *him* particularly. He was ten years younger than Mummy, and a bit of a flirt.'

Olivia swallowed hard, completely stunned by what Sally had told her. It seemed that Marcus's reconciliation with his wife had not only failed, but that Ruth had also divorced him and married someone else. Heavens, no wonder he was in torment!

'Still, Mummy seemed happy enough with him.' Sally got up off the bed. 'I really wish you were staying, Olivia,' she added softly. 'Daddy doesn't know what he's doing by dismissing you.'

'Oh, I think he does,' Olivia sighed softly. 'I've been like a barb in his side ever since I came here,' and after what Sally had just told her she might have been more so than she had ever imagined. Twice Marcus had called out in his sleep begging Ruth to come back to him, denying he had ever wanted or needed a girl called Olivia. She knew she had to be that Olivia, could it be that she had been instrumental in his reconciliation with Ruth failing? Sybil Carr had warned her six years ago that Ruth wouldn't care for the fact that Marcus had been amusing himself with a little nurse. She had also accused him, only hours ago, of forcing Ruth into another man's arms.

Olivia knew she would have to leave here, the possibility that Marcus would one day realise she was the Olivia who had made Ruth leave was something that could seriously harm him in his condition. She had told him she would leave in the morning, and that was exactly what she would do. But not before she had seen him once more.

Her dinner remained uneaten on the tray Sally had brought up to her room, the thought of sitting at the same table with Sybil Carr after the accusations she had made totally unpalatable to her. The deliciously cooked food held no appeal for her either, and the time dragged by slowly until she felt sure Marcus would be asleep, knowing this was the only way she would get to see him again.

The light had once again been left on in his room, but the man on the bed was fast asleep, only a sheet pulled up over his naked torso, a pair of black pyjama trousers resting low down on his hips. Olivia had seen him like this numerous times during the weeks she had been working here, but he still made her breath catch in her throat at his male beauty. He was much leaner than he had been six years ago, but he was still tautly muscled, and exuded an aura of power that made her fingertips tremble as she lightly touched his chest. Her hand moved away as if she had been burnt as he stirred restlessly in his sleep, relaxing once again as he merely turned over and away from her as she sat on the side of the bed.

'I never meant to hurt you, Marcus,' she told him softly, able to tell him exactly how she felt now that he was asleep and so couldn't hear her. 'I never meant to make you feel less of a man, I would have gladly shared your bed if I had once thought you really cared for me. Oh, darling, I—I've never stopped caring for you, not even when you hurt me so badly,' her voice broke emotionally. 'I wish you *had* been my lover, Marcus,' she added achingly. 'At least then I should have something to remember, something good between us.'

Her tears fell unbidden as she continued to look down at the leanly muscled back of the man she loved, unable to resist the urge to touch him yet again, loving the ripple of power beneath her fingertips, smooth skin only lightly covered with dark hair, his chest more so, the hair there thick and wiry.

'If you ever do want me, ever need me,' she began to talk again, softly, so as not to disturb him, 'I'll always be here.' She stood up reluctantly, turning to leave, knowing that if she didn't go now then she wouldn't go at all. And she couldn't bear his derision if she gave in to the impulse to share his bed.

Her own room seemed cold and lonely, and she climbed miserably beneath the covers, the pillow beneath her muffling the sound of her sobbing. She had known that to come here would cause her pain, and it was a pain that was tenfold what she had felt six years ago. She didn't even know where she was going tomorrow when she left here—and she didn't really care either. She had never felt such helplessness with life before.

'Olivia.'

She froze at the sound of that voice, turning slowly to see Marcus standing in the doorway. She blinked hard, sure she was imagining things.

'Can I come in?' he requested huskily.

She hadn't imagined him at all, he really was here. She gave him a panicked look—had he been awake all the time, had he heard the things she said as she said goodbye to him?

'I woke up a few minutes ago and couldn't get back to sleep.' His words reassured her that he hadn't. 'I had to come and say goodbye to you. I'm sure you weren't going to come to me before you left in the morning,' he added derisively. 'Were you?' he prompted at her silence.

Olivia moistened her lips, uncertain how to answer him, not even sure that she could.

'Would you mind if I come in?' he repeated softly. 'I wouldn't want Sybil to indulge in her nocturnal wanderings and jump to the wrong conclusions again,' he added mockingly.

Her spine stiffened, and she sat up suddenly. 'Please, come in,' she invited disjointedly. 'If you think we have any more to say to each other.' She held her breath as he came in and closed the door behind him, terrified he might not think they had and walked away.

'Don't worry,' he taunted as he walked surely to the side of the bed, his only clothing still the pair of black pyjama trousers, his hair tousled from sleep. 'I haven't come to try and persuade you into not leaving.' His mouth twisted. 'We both know I no longer need that constant attention.'

Olivia swallowed hard. 'Yes.'

'But there's something I do need.'

'Yes?' She instantly cursed herself for her eagerness, chewing on her bottom lip. 'Er—What's that?'

Marcus sat on the side of her bed, leaning forward, his hands moving lightly up her arms, across her bare shoulders to cup her face. 'I wish I could see you,' he muttered with a sigh. 'You're beautiful, aren't you?'

'No——'

'Yes, you are,' he said roughly. 'I asked Sally weeks ago and she told me you are. Your hair is like a flame shot through with sunlight, your skin is smooth and creamy, and you have eyes the colour of the deepest emeralds, big eyes that totally dominate your face. And a mouth that I *ache* to kiss!'

Olivia's breath left her in a gasp. 'Marcus ... .'

'Do you have any idea how much I've longed to kiss you?' he continued as if she hadn't spoken. 'How much I've *needed* to kiss you?' His voice roughened. 'But you've always been so damned efficient, so much the nurse. Is there a woman in there?' he mocked.

'You know there is,' she groaned, feeling weak. 'You once came here and spent the night with me.'

'Only part of it,' he reminded her harshly. 'You threw me out.'

'I had to.'

'Are you going to throw me out tonight too?' he rasped.

'Your mother-in-law——'

'Damn Sybil!' he dismissed raggedly. 'Are you going to send me away?'

She trembled beneath his touch, totally mesmerised by the hard beauty of his face in the moonlight as he looked down at her, tense as he waited for her reply. 'No,' she gave the only answer she could.

'Olivia?' Marcus prompted her barely discernible reply.

'I said no!' Her voice was raised almost angrily. 'No, I won't send you away,' she repeated raggedly. 'I won't ever send you away. Don't you know that yet?'

'Kiss me, Olivia,' he demanded arrogantly. 'If you don't soon kiss me I'm going to go insane!'

With a choked cry she raised her mouth to his, instantly feeling his response as his lips opened over hers. The kiss was deep and intimate, Marcus's hands knowledgeable on her shoulders as she slid the ribbon straps of her nightgown down her arms, the silky material falling down about her waist. She gasped as one of his hands gently cupped her breast, and an ache built deep within her as he continued to caress her, probing the sensitivity of her lips until with a groan he lowered her back on to the bed. Olivia clung to the broadness of his shoulders in a world that had suddenly gone wild, only Marcus himself seeming like reality.

'You're beautiful,' he murmured gratingly as he kissed his way slowly down her throat, his hand leaving her breast now as his mouth paid homage to its beauty, kissing every silken inch before taking the deep red tip between his lips, holding her beneath him with ease as passion ripped through her body, cupping her other breast before that too received the same intense caresses. 'So beautiful,' he muttered on the journey down the taut flatness of her stomach, as he dispatched her nightgown to the floor, his lips and hands knowing her body better than his eyes ever could. But it still wasn't enough for him, and he swore under his breath as she arched in ecstasy, her head thrown back in abandon. 'God, how I wish I could see you,' he rasped. 'Wish I could see how you look with your hair spread out across the pillow, your eyes passion-drugged—for me.'

'It isn't important——'

'To me it is!'

'No,' she insisted firmly, coming up on her knees beside him, framing his dearly-loved face with tender hands. 'Let me show you,' she begged.

'Another lesson in psychology?' he snapped his bitterness.

'I won't let you do this to us again, Marcus,' she told him determinedly.

'Do what to us?' He lay back on the pillow, his eyes closed, deep lines grooved beside his nose and mouth. 'I was a fool to come here. Do you let all your patients make love to you to ease their tension?' he scorned.

She held on to her own temper with effort, knowing he was deliberately trying to anger her. And this time she wasn't going to let him do it. 'Why should I exclude them when the doctors have that privilege?' She watched as he flinched. 'I'm only telling you what you wanted to hear, Marcus. Only you see it isn't true,' her voice softened. 'No doctor, no patient, no *one* has ever made love to me,' she told him clearly. 'I've never wanted anyone to make love to me—until

now. I want you, Marcus, and I'm going to make love
to you.'

'Olivia——'

'Don't try and stop me.' She pushed his hands back
to his sides. 'I may not be too good at this, I don't
have the experience, but I'm sure you won't find me
lacking in enthusiasm,' she added tremulously.

'Olivia!' Marcus groaned again.

'For God's sake don't make me beg!' she pleaded,
watching the play of emotions on his face as the fight
went out of him, the grooves beside his mouth easing
as he visibly relaxed.

But he didn't stay relaxed for long once she began to
caress him, his body arching towards her as her hands
became bolder, his breathing ragged as her lips moved
across the flatness of his stomach to his taut thighs.

'Dear God!' he groaned as her warmth enveloped
him, his breath leaving him in a shuddering sigh.

Olivia loved the taste and feel of him, loved the
increasing power she had over his body, although she
had to gasp her own pleasure as she felt his hands once
again caressing her breasts. She moaned her disappointment as Marcus gently lifted her up on to his
body.

'I can't take any more of that,' he told her ruefully, a
sensual curve to his lips. 'And you're right, Olivia, I
don't need to see your body to enjoy it.' He lifted her
up towards him until he could lower one of her breasts
into his mouth, gently sucking on the hardened nipple,
the soft whimpering sounds Olivia heard amazingly
coming from her own lips. 'That's how a child would
feel suckling from you,' he said huskily. 'Have you
ever wanted a child, Olivia?'

'Every woman wants children,' she told him
raggedly, shaken at the thought of possibly having
Marcus's child.

'And you would look beautiful too. You have such

an exciting body, darling.' Marcus rolled over so that she was beneath him, kissing her all the way down the body he liked so much, from the curves of her ears to the soles of her feet, chuckling softly at the tension that ran through her as he kissed each toe.

'It tickles,' she complained breathlessly.

'Liar!' He gave a throaty laugh, before making a slow journey back up her calf, her knees, her thighs, groaning his satisfaction as he claimed the scented sweetness of her.

'Oh, Marcus, Marcus . . .!' She couldn't seem to stop shaking as she clung to him.

'Are you ready for me now, darling?'

'Yes. Oh yes!' She grasped his shoulders as he moved between her parted thighs, bracing himself above her before possessing her with a fierceness cloaked in gentleness, remaining suddenly still as he met the tiny barrier to his full lovemaking.

He raised his head dazedly, still positioned over her, taking his weight off her on to his elbows. 'My God, you really meant——! Olivia?' he questioned raggedly.

'Please!' she groaned her need for that final possession. 'Please, Marcus!' With an arch of her hips she was the one to make that final move that made her one with him, moaning at the slight pain she felt.

'*God!*' Marcus blinked his surprise. 'Dear God!' His breathing was heavy in his disbelief. 'Olivia!' He framed her face, looking down at her.

She moistened suddenly dry lips. 'You aren't going to stop now?'

'No, I'm not going to stop now.' He kissed her with a savagery that made her open her mouth to his, his body moving against and inside her with a thrust that soon had them gasping their mutual desire, Olivia hardly able to believe this second, more intense ecstasy, clinging to him as exhaustion quickly claimed her, while Marcus lay beside her, her head resting against his chest.

CHAPTER TEN

AFTER a night of being held in Marcus's arms the bed seemed strangely empty without him. Olivia came awake slowly, reluctantly, knowing she was alone in the narrow bed, missing the warm roughness of Marcus's legs entwined with hers, the soft movement of his chest as he breathed beneath her.

Marcus had gone, but the feel of his lovemaking lingered on in the lethargy of her body, her still sensitive skin. They had slept for a long time after their first ecstatic lovemaking, Olivia revelling in the dizzying pleasure of being in his arms. Then towards dawn she had woken to the sure caress of gentle hands on her body, groaning her eagerness as he would have moved away from her, kissing him deeply even in her half-asleep state. The second time Marcus made love to her he had been even more gentle, conscious of her tender flesh, the slow even thrusts of his body quickly sending them both into spasms of delight.

She knew that she well and truly belonged to him now, that during the all-too-short hours of the night he had become an even more important part of her life—and she hadn't believed that was possible. But she had no idea how Marcus really felt about her, whether she had just been a female body to him, or if she meant something more to him. Their murmured words had only been ones of appreciation, of pleasure, and the word love definitely hadn't been mentioned by either of them.

But she didn't care! She had wanted to belong to Marcus, now had that memory of him to cherish for ever. Even if she never saw him again she could never forget him.

She surfaced above the tangled sheets as a knock sounded on the door, blinking the sleep from her fogged brain as Sally bounced into the room.

The young girl looked in astonishment at the bedraggled bedclothes, her brows rising even more as she saw Olivia make a grab for her nightgown off the floor. 'Had a bad night?' she frowned.

Hot colour flooded Olivia's cheeks, knowing the evidence was very damning. Oh well, Sally was far from being a child any more. 'No, as a matter of fact I've had a very good night,' she answered coolly, sitting up to pull her nightgown on over her head, before getting out of bed to brush the knots from her hair.

'Olivia?'

'Have you seen your father this morning?' She refused to meet the question in Sally's eyes.

'Yes,' she grimaced. 'He's snapping and snarling at everyone,' she explained.

Olivia's hand shook slightly as she returned the hairbrush to the dressing-table.

'Simon is with him at the moment,' Sally continued lightly.

It was still early, only nine-thirty. 'Is he feeling ill?' Could last night have been too much for him?

The younger girl shrugged. 'Don't ask me, Daddy never tell me anything.'

'And Simon?'

'He just quotes professional etiquette at me,' Sally sighed.

Olivia chewed on her bottom lip, sure that something must be wrong for Marcus to have called Simon out this early. 'Your father is—all right?'

'He looks a little tired,' Sally told her pointedly. 'But otherwise, yes. Are you still leaving this morning?'

'Unless your father has changed his mind—and I

don't think he has.' Olivia sat down heavily on the bedroom chair, aware that she too had hoped last night had altered things between herself and Marcus. It seemed it hadn't.

'Olivia . . .?'

'Yes?' She forced herself to meet questioning grey eyes, and then wished she hadn't as she was instantly aware of Sally's likeness to her father.

'Daddy spent the night in here last night, didn't he?' Sally seemed reluctant to pry with the question, although her mutinous expression demanded an answer, a truthful one.

Olivia swallowed hard, moistening her lips with the tip of her tongue, lips that still tingled from the often fierce pleasure of Marcus's. She lingered over the taste of him there, then looked up to find Sally watching her compassionately. 'It would be useless to deny it, wouldn't it?' she smiled shakily.

'Why should you want to?'

'I don't—particularly. Although I do want you to know that what your grandmother said wasn't true. Your father and I have not been having an affair all the time I've been here, last night was—well, it was an impulsive thing, something that had never happened before. And going to bed with someone doesn't necessarily solve any problems,' she sighed. 'Men feel differently about these things from women, and——'

'I know all about that,' the girl dismissed with some of her father's impatient arrogance. 'But I hope you aren't trying to tell me that my father spent the night with you, made love with you, and that it meant nothing to him. I don't believe that!'

'Sally——'

'Daddy felt very strongly about you six years ago, I don't think that's changed.'

Olivia sighed at Sally's stubborn tone, knowing it must be difficult for her to accept that her father was as human as other men. 'He doesn't even remember me, Sally.' She thought of the times he had talked about her from his subconscious. 'Well, not consciously, anyway.'

'I'm not sure I believe that either.' Sally shook her head.

'Whether you believe it or not won't change the fact that I'm leaving this morning.'

'We'll see about that!' Sally told her determinedly, walking to the door. 'I'm going to talk to Daddy about it.'

Olivia made no effort to stop her leaving, knowing that once she heard the truth from Marcus Sally would have to believe it. She didn't even care if Marcus was angry with her for telling Sally about their night together—it had happened, nothing could ever change that.

She dressed in close-fitting black trousers and a bottle green vest-top, putting the finishing touches to her packing when her bedroom door was flung open without warning. Expecting an angry Marcus, she was surprised to see Sybil Carr standing there, her narrow-eyed gaze raking over her with arrogant disdain.

'So you really are leaving, Miss King.' She came further into the room. 'Realising for a second time that you have no part in Marcus's life?'

Olivia stiffened at the insulting tone, straightening to look at the other woman unflinchingly. 'Marcus no longer needs a nurse, no.'

'Or a mistress!' Sybil scorned.

'Mrs Carr——'

'Marcus tired of you even quicker than last time, didn't he?' Sybil mocked, the blue eyes hard. 'He tired of Ruth in the same way,' she added angrily.

'The first or second time?' asked Olivia wearily, tired of the emotional scenes she had to face in this house. Perhaps she would be glad to get away after all.

'What second—Oh, you mean the reconciliation!' Sybil gave a hard laugh. 'Have you been sharing Marcus's bed all these weeks and not yet realised there was no reconciliation?'

Olivia felt as if she must have swayed, and reached blindly behind her for the bedroom chair, badly shaken. 'But you told me—You said on the telephone——' She was having difficulty articulating through her suddenly parched lips. 'That night I called the house to speak to Marcus you told me he and your daughter were back together, that they were getting ready to go out.'

Sybil sighed. 'I don't suppose what I tell you now is going to do any harm, even if you run and tell Marcus it won't change anything. Your explanation is six years too late, and Marcus isn't the most forgiving of men. I told you that night what you expected to hear. You didn't even want to talk to Marcus when I offered to call him,' she scorned sneeringly.

'But Ruth *was* there,' Olivia said dazedly. 'I *saw* her!'

'Possibly,' Sybil nodded distantly. 'Sally was involved in an accident, she was knocked over on her way home from school. Ruth came back from France to be with her.'

'Not—not with Marcus?'

'No,' the other woman gave a mirthless laugh. 'I knew the moment he introduced you to me that he was serious about you.' Her eyes glittered her dislike. 'A little nobody like you going to take my daughter's place!' She shook her head. 'I couldn't have that.'

Olivia felt sick, hardly able to think straight. 'Then you never told Marcus I'd telephoned?'

'Oh, I told him,' Sybil gave an unpleasant smile. 'I told him what he expected to hear too—that you'd realised he was too old for you, that you couldn't cope with the fact that he already had a wife and young child, that you didn't have the courage to tell him yourself, that you never wanted to see him again.'

Olivia's eyes were huge in her pale face, knowing that both she and Marcus had played into this woman's hands perfectly. 'He believed you?' she choked.

'Why not?' Sybil shrugged. 'You believed me when I told you he and Ruth were back together. God, you were such a naïve child, running away like you did. Apparently by the time Sally had convalesced enough to return to school you'd left the hospital, had requested a transfer. Marcus needed no further confirmation that it was over between the two of you.'

'Oh God!' Olivia buried her face in her hands, finally giving in to her shocked tears.

'It was like a nightmare to me the day you came back from the hospital with Sally,' the other woman continued remorselessly. 'But my fears that you and Marcus would realise the truth never materialised. You're no more sure of each other now than you were then!'

'Marcus doesn't even remember me from six years ago,' Olivia cried, living the nightmare of knowing she had been wrong about him all these years, that he had never taken Ruth back.

'I've never forgotten you.' He spoke gruffly from the open doorway, walking across the room to her side, the dark glasses once again shielding his expressive eyes. 'For six years I've believed you never really cared for me, that you——' he broke off, too angry to continue, his eyes glacial as he turned to his mother-in-law. 'I think you need a long holiday, Sybil,' he rasped. 'Far away from me—and Olivia.'

'Marcus——'

'I think you should leave,' he said tautly, unmoved by her shocked paleness.

'But——'

'I'm sure Sally and Simon would be glad to get you a taxi,' he continued hardly. 'I would advise that you leave it at least a year before even thinking of coming near me again.'

'But where will I go?' she gasped.

'I hope to the hell you've made me suffer for the last six years!' A pulse beat erratically in his clenched jaw.

Olivia watched as the other woman stormed out of the room, slamming the door behind her, before turning dazed green eyes on Marcus. 'You've known it was me all the time?' she groaned.

'Yes,' he nodded, his hands thrust deep into the pockets of his grey trousers, moving away from her now that they were alone, his shoulders rigid. 'But I was blind! Sally came back from a pool party to tell me that she'd seen you again, that you were as beautiful as ever. I was called out to an emergency that evening and all I could think of was you, how beautiful you were, how much I wanted to see you again. I was still thinking of you as I drove home later that evening, needed to see you again so badly I didn't notice the truck until it was too late——'

'It was my fault you crashed!' she realised with a gasp.

'No, my fault,' he corrected deeply, his back rigid as he turned away from her. 'I was filled with self-doubt, desperate to come to you and yet frightened of rejection after all these years, sure you would turn me away. I'm convinced my blindness was my way of evading facing that possibility, a way of telling myself I *couldn't* come to you. When I regained consciousness after the accident I believed I was hallucinating that you were there, knew you couldn't really be.'

Olivia could only stare at his back, too disturbed to even be able to answer him coherently.

'As the time passed, days, weeks, I knew I must

have imagined you were ever there, that I'd wanted you to be so much, had cried out to you that it was you I had always loved and not Ruth, that I had forced you to appear in my mind, and only in my mind. I daren't even mention it to Sally for fear that she *would* think I was losing my mind.'

Olivia couldn't believe it—Marcus had been calling out for *her* not to leave him, not Ruth, she had just misunderstood his mumbled pleadings.

'And then you were there again,' he rubbed his nape. 'Taunting me, tormenting me, giving me a reason to live when I didn't want one.'

'Marcus!'

'Wasn't that what Sally told you when she begged you to come and see me?' he jeered. 'That I'd given up, that I wanted to die?'

'She didn't beg me, and I—I wanted to come.'

'Why?' He turned suddenly, seeming to look at her across the room. 'God, the torment the day you arrived here as my nurse and I Brailled you,' he groaned. 'You felt so good, I could have taken you then. Would you have let me? It has to be the truth between us now, Olivia,' he rasped. 'You see, it isn't too late, as Sybil said, it could never be too late for you. I've told you I never forgot you, did you ever forget me?'

Olivia swallowed hard. 'I tried,' she said huskily. 'And sometimes I did manage to put you out of my mind for days at a time. But I could never forget you completely.'

'Why not?' Marcus persisted.

'You were the first man I ever loved——'

'The *first?*' he rasped harshly.

She looked down at her hands. 'And the last. I loved you six years ago, completely, utterly, and when you said we had to think about our relationship, to talk about it, I believed I would finally be able to tell you how I felt. When you cancelled our date without explanation for the next evening, and then the next day I saw you at the hospital with Ruth——'

'It was at the hospital you saw us?' he frowned.

'Yes,' she admitted heavily. 'You seemed engrossed in each other, happy to be together, and when I telephoned the house Sybil told me you were going out for the evening, that you were back together.'

'Ruth and I were happy together that evening because Sally had been in intensive care since the afternoon before, she'd been on the critical list, and we'd just learnt that she was going to be all right. I wanted to share that happiness with you, to be with you, and then Sybil told me about your call.' His mouth tightened ominously. 'I could have committed murder that night! I thought the best thing to do was to give you time,' he sighed. 'After all, you were very young, and I knew that the existence of Ruth and Sally had bothered you, that the adult love I had for you was perhaps more than you could handle at that time. I took Sally away on a long convalescence to her mother, and when I got back you'd transferred to another hospital. That seemed pretty conclusive as to what you'd decided was best for you.'

'But it wasn't!' She shook her head, groaning at the misunderstandings that had separated them then—that could still separate them? 'I just knew I couldn't go on working in the same hospital as you now that you were back with your wife.'

Marcus gave a deep sigh. 'Why did you agree to come here as my nurse? Was it to torment me, as I thought, to pay me back for once wanting you?'

'No!' she cried, standing up. '*I'm* the one who's been in torment having to work with you like this. But you seemed to need me, reacted only to me. Don't you know I would do anything to help you?'

Marcus seemed to stiffen. 'Anything?'

'Yes!'

'Does that include making love to a blind man?' he rasped.

'*No!*' she gasped. 'That wasn't to help you, that was for *me*.'

'Then you did mean what you said last night?'

'What I said?' she repeated uncertainly.

'That you'd never stopped caring for me?' He waited tensely for her reply.

'You were awake?' Her eyes were wide.

'All the time,' he nodded. 'I'd had to tell you to go, how could I possibly sleep? And then when you came to my room, touched me, said the things you did, I knew I couldn't let you go without making love to you.'

Delicate colour heated her cheeks. 'Then you must know it's the truth,' she choked.

'Why were you a virgin, Olivia?' he persisted relentlessly.

She turned away, her breathing ragged. 'I told you, I never wanted another man.'

'And I never wanted another woman, not since the first day I met you. There's been no one else all these years, Olivia.'

She spun round at the softly spoken words, seeing that amazingly all the tension had left him, that he was actually smiling. 'Marcus?' she queried tentatively.

He came towards her with confident strides, talking as he walked. 'I used to torture myself imagining you with other lovers, possibly with a husband, children.' He came to a halt in front of her, their bodies almost touching, their warmth reaching out to each other. 'And then Sally came home and told me that you didn't even have a boy-friend, let alone a husband! I'm afraid she asked Rick for that bit of information,' he smiled down as she gasped. 'I at once began hoping, praying that I could mean something to you again.

When I realised I was blind I daren't even acknowledge that I remembered you. Yours is the sort of kind heart that makes sacrifices, and I knew that if you once guessed how much I needed you . . .' His mouth twisted. 'But I'm afraid you've been a temptation to me ever since you came here, a temptation I couldn't always resist. I'm sorry if I've hurt you with my cruelty, Olivia.'

She forgave him every single second of pain in that moment. 'Tell me—tell me——'

'Yes?' he prompted as she chewed awkwardly on her bottom lip.

She looked up at him fearlessly. 'How *did* you feel about me six years ago?'

'Haven't I just told you?'

'Not completely, no,' she gave a shaky laugh.

Marcus gave a rueful grimace. 'No, maybe I haven't. Before I do perhaps I should do the explaining about Ruth that should have been made then, then you would never have doubted me. You overheard Sybil yesterday when she accused me of marrying Ruth for the wrong reasons?' He sighed as she nodded confirmation. 'She was right. Ruth was beautiful, an accomplished hostess—and we both married for reasons other than love. She enjoyed being the wife of the brilliant surgeon everyone assured her I was going to be, and I wanted a wife who would complement that position. Unfortunately, no one had told Ruth that it would take me years to reach the top of my field, and I hadn't realised how galling it was going to be to have a wife whose father would buy her anything she asked for. By the time Sally was born we were living almost as strangers. But I loved my daughter very much, and I was determined to keep the family together. I succeeded until Pierre came along.'

'Sally told me about her stepfather.'

Surprise widened his eyes, and then he nodded

acceptance of the fact that his daughter had confided in her. 'At first I thought we should try and patch our marriage up, and then I realised that it wasn't a marriage at all but a business arrangement. I realised that the day I went on to a ward to visit one of my patients and a girl with eyes big enough for me to drown in walked straight into my arms!'

'You looked straight through me!' Olivia accused with indignation. 'And I was mortified.'

'I looked into your eyes—very much as I'm doing now—and I fell in love with you.'

'Marcus?' His name came out as a high-pitched squeak, searching the harshness of his face, wishing she could see behind the dark glasses. 'Did you say you could—see me?' She swallowed hard.

'Would it matter to you if I'm still blind?'

'I wouldn't care if you were blind, had six wives and twenty children—I love you, I've always loved you.'

'I think I knew that last night as I made love to you. The moment you gave me your innocence was the moment I realised that you loved me—and it was the moment I began to see again!' he told her exultantly. 'I thought you would have forgotten me the last years, pushed what we had to the back of your mind, and then there you were giving me the innocence I had wanted six years ago! Something inside me snapped with the joy I felt at that moment, the restraint was all gone, and I looked down and I could—I could suddenly see you, your beauty, your fire.'

'Why didn't you tell me?' She touched his cheek wonderingly, now knowing the reason for the dark glasses. The stark daylight was too glaring for his sensitive sight.

'I had other things on my mind at the time,' he teased softly. 'No,' he sobered, 'that wasn't it, although God knows at the time nothing was more important to me than loving you. I had to be sure, darling, that the return of my sight wasn't just temporary. No matter how much I love you, how much I've always loved you, I couldn't inflict you with a blind husband.'

'You wouldn't have been inflicting—*Husband?*' she repeated incredulously.

Marcus gently framed her face with loving hands. 'My darling, will you marry me?'

'I ought to be angry with you, not marry you!' She glared up at him. 'How dare you insult me by thinking I would go to bed with you, want to marry you, out of pity?'

'I couldn't offer you less than you deserve, Olivia,' he told her throatily.

'But it didn't matter to me!'

'It mattered to me,' he said quietly.

Olivia frowned. 'Are you saying that if you were still blind you would have let me leave here today, even though you love me?'

'I don't know,' he told her truthfully. 'You see, until I overheard Sybil and the lies she once told us I believed you had walked out on me six years ago. If I were still blind, and had learnt the truth, I have no idea what my reaction would have been. Give me the benefit of the doubt, hm?' he chided softly.

She looked up at him with love in her eyes, realising how close they had come to losing each other again, and she put her arms about his waist to rest her head on his chest. 'You can see again, will be completely well again—that's all that matters.' She spoke into the silk of his shirt.

'And are you going to marry me?'

'I'll think about it.'

'Six years wasn't long enough?' he joined in her light teasing.

Her arms tightened about him. 'I think I knew I loved you the moment I accidentally turned into your arms too, darling.' Her head went back as she gave him a dazzling smile. 'Yes, I'll marry you.' She and Marcus had the same everlasting love the Batesons had shared, they both knew it and would cherish it.

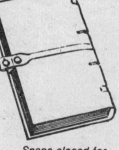

Take these 4 best-selling novels FREE

Yes! Four sophisticated, contemporary love stories by four world-famous authors of romance FREE, as your introduction to the Harlequin Presents subscription plan. Thrill to **Anne Mather**'s passionate story BORN OUT OF LOVE, set in the Caribbean.... Travel to darkest Africa in **Violet Winspear**'s TIME OF THE TEMPTRESS.... Let **Charlotte Lamb** take you to the fascinating world of London's Fleet Street in MAN'S WORLD.... Discover beautiful Greece in **Sally Wentworth**'s moving romance SAY HELLO TO YESTERDAY.

Harlequin Presents...

The very finest in romance fiction

Join the millions of avid Harlequin readers all over the world who delight in the magic of a really exciting novel. EIGHT great NEW titles published EACH MONTH! Each month you will get to know exciting, interesting, true-to-life people .... You'll be swept to distant lands you've dreamed of visiting .... Intrigue, adventure, romance, and the destiny of many lives will thrill you through each Harlequin Presents novel.

Get all the latest books before they're sold out!
As a Harlequin subscriber you actually receive your personal copies of the latest Presents novels immediately after they come off the press, so you're sure of getting all 8 each month.

Cancel your subscription whenever you wish!
You don't have to buy any minimum number of books. Whenever you decide to stop your subscription just let us know and we'll cancel all further shipments.

Yours FREE, with a home subscription to
HARLEQUIN SUPERROMANCE T.M.

Now you never have to miss reading the newest HARLEQUIN SUPERROMANCES... because they'll be delivered right to your door.

Start with your **FREE** LOVE BEYOND DESIRE. You'll be enthralled by this powerful love story...from the moment Robin meets the dark, handsome Carlos and finds herself involved in the jealousies, bitterness and secret passions of the Lopez family. Where her own forbidden love threatens to shatter her life.

Your **FREE** LOVE BEYOND DESIRE is only the beginning. A subscription to HARLEQUIN SUPERROMANCE lets you look forward to a long love affair. Month after month, you'll receive four love stories of heroic dimension. Novels that will involve you in spellbinding intrigue, forbidden love and fiery passions.

You'll begin this series of sensuous, exciting contemporary novels...written by some of the top romance novelists of the day...with four every month.

And this big value...each novel, almost 400 pages of compelling reading...is yours for only $2.50 a book. Hours of entertainment every month for so little. Far less than a first-run movie or pay-TV. Newly published novels, with beautifully illustrated covers, filled with page after page of delicious escape into a world of romantic love...delivered right to your home.

Begin a long love affair with

HARLEQUIN SUPERROMANCE.™

Accept LOVE BEYOND DESIRE **FREE**.

Complete and mail the coupon below today!

- -